KING OF TEMPTATION

LORDS OF LAS VEGAS

TAMMY ANDRESEN

Created with Vellum

KING OF TEMPTATION

A cruel baby daddy billionaire boss.

A desperate college coed who has run out of options.

Ruthless
Lethal
Arrogant
Handsome as sin

The Kincaid family rules Vegas and Leo Kincaid is their fist...the enforcer with a temper that makes most men tremble.

I should have run when I had the chance.

But when sexy AF Leo offers me one night of passion, I take it. That's the thing about a guy who runs hot...being with him is like nothing I've ever known before.

What could go wrong?

Turns out, everything. Because that is the moment my life falls apart and Leo is the reason. He is the fist. And it's my life he bashes into tiny pieces...starting with my dream to be a professional ballet dancer.

But I can't leave this city without money.

So, I do something I never imagined, and I apply for a job as a cage dancer at Temptation, one of the hottest clubs on the Strip.

But that doesn't help me escape Leo. Far from it. Because Temptation is his club, which makes him my new boss. He's got me well and truly under his heel. Could my life get any worse?

Why yes, yes it can. Not only is Leo Kincaid my one-night stand, the reason my life fell apart, and my new boss, but he's the fist. And men who go around bashing people get hit back. His enemies are coming for him—and for me.

And I'm not sure I can escape. Because...

Leo's got one more title in my life. Baby daddy.

I just found out I'm pregnant.

Welcome to the Dark side of Las Vegas where the stakes are even higher and the men more lethal... *King of Sinners* if the first book in the "Lords of Las Vegas" series, but don't worry... there will be more! Coming soon...

King of Sinners
King of Temptation
King of Wrath
King of Pain
King of Ruin

STALK ME LIKE AN ALPHA!

Join my newsletter to get all the latest updates!

Tammy's Newsletter

And follow me everywhere else for teasers, giveaway, book news and fun!

www.authortammyandresen.com
www.facebook.com/authortammyandresen
www.instagram.com/tammyandresen
https://www.tiktok.com/@lordsoflasvegas
www://amazon.com/authortammyandresen

CHAPTER ONE

Kim

"It's almost disgusting," I mutter to myself as I look out the window at the picturesque mountains beyond.

The morning of Charlotte and Mason's wedding is a perfect Colorado spring day. It rained last night—I could hear it on the roof—but today, the world is bright and shiny for the washing it received the night before.

The grass is a brilliant green, the sky a bright blue dotted with white puffy clouds, the Aspen pines a perfect shade of dark green.

I stare out the window of the honeymoon suite I shared with my best friend Charlotte and marvel at the perfection. When you have money, even nature works to please you.

We're at some high-end hotel and resort in Aspen, the sort where I've never even dreamed of staying. One night probably costs more than my whole month's rent. I don't know because Charlotte's fiancé, Mason, paid for my flight here and my room, along with all the extras.

Which is crazy to me, I'm not even using the room he paid for since I kept Charlotte company last night. I keep track of every penny —I have to—and waste is currently not in my vocabulary.

This room is twice the size of my apartment in Las Vegas, and I share that place with three other dancers.

This wedding is a lavish display of wealth that makes my head spin.

But the money is not what unsettles me deep down. The Kincaid men, all five of them, have jangled my nerves. They are all handsome as sin, with their dark hair and their piercing brown eyes. Each of them is as rich as they are successful.

But they all have this edge. You can feel it under the surface.

Dangerous.

They are as intoxicating as they are nerve wracking and I've been jittery since I got here. Especially when the second Kincaid brother enters the room, Leo. He's more of everything.

More muscles, more good looks, more sinister charm that sets my pulse fluttering and my gaze darting about the room. There is something so deliciously dangerous about him.

Which is a reaction I can ill afford. I'm so close to realizing my dreams, I cannot allow a distraction now, no matter how tempting.

It's crazy to me that my best friend is marrying one of these predators. I'd be more worried about Charlotte and what she's getting into, except Mason seems to worship her.

And by extension, he's lavished me with gifts. Plane ticket, room, dress, spa day.

I wouldn't have been able to come if he hadn't. I have exactly enough money to pay for myself to fly from here to New York tomorrow morning to attend my interview with the New York City Ballet and not a penny more if I'm going to pay rent this month.

In fact, I'm pretty sure I'm going to have to sleep in the airport before my return flight the day after tomorrow.

But I don't care about that. This interview is a dream come true and my one chance at having the career no one from my childhood would ever have imagined for me. The one my mother dreamed of and never got the chance to have because she had me instead.

Charlotte is still asleep as I sit by the window, staring at the lush garden below, the staff already hard at work making the perfect garden even better for the upcoming ceremony.

The gazebo is decorated with a gauzy fabric that floats in the morning breeze while white chairs are set at perfectly angled rows.

A little sigh escapes my lips. I might be cautious around the Kincaids, but I'm still a bit jealous about the way they live.

I shake off that feeling. I'm going to hold to the plan for a little while longer to make my dreams come true.

A soft knock sounds at the door, and I get up to answer it, tightening the lush robe around my waist, before I crack the door open.

Mason is standing on the other side. He's the picture of business casual, masculine elegance this morning. With his pressed slacks and his white shirt that is tucked in but open a single button at the collar.

I've never been into guys who are that perfectly coiffed, not a hair out of place, but I can't deny he cuts quite the figure.

Charlotte did well. Though, I always knew she would. Stunningly gorgeous, quiet and shy, she has this demure grace that makes men like Mason froth. Charlotte and I waited tables together at a bar called Rebel's. The serious businessmen who came in always gave Charlotte a long look.

"Morning," I whisper.

"Good morning," he murmurs back. "Charlotte still asleep?"

I nod. "Yeah. I can wake her if you want."

"No," he shakes his head. "I just wanted to know how she slept."

Man, oh man, this guy's got it bad. I duck my head to hide my smile, a different touch of envy settling in my chest. What would it be like to have someone care for me like this? The idea of not struggling quite so hard makes me ache deep down to think it.

But with my gaze cast down, I almost miss the fact that Leo has appeared until he's right next to Mason. When I look up to speak to Mason, Leo's there, his cocking grin and deep brown eyes holding mine and I feel a blush climb my cheeks as our gazes connect.

If Mason is too coiffed, Leo is the exact brand of sexy that makes my brain fritz. He's got on a fitted T-shirt and tight jeans that show off his many, many muscles.

Bulkier and rougher than his brother, he looks like trouble in the best way possible. Not that I'm looking for problems, but if I were…

My gaze snaps back to Mason, who is scowling at Leo. Charlotte mentioned tension between the two brothers and I feel it now.

Leo hardens at his brother's stare, the sexy smile disappearing.

Clearing my throat, I give Mason a bright smile. "We went to bed early, promise." I draw an X over my heart to illustrate my point, hoping to distract from whatever is happening in front of me.

Mason's gaze returns to me, softening. "Thanks, Kim. Don't forget to go to the desk and get a key for your room tonight. I've also arranged for a car to take you to the airport tomorrow morning so you don't have worry about that either. If there is anything else you need, don't hesitate to ask. Now or in the future."

I nod as I look the other way, not meeting the gaze of either Kincaid. "Thank you, Mason. I really appreciate it." My dad was never around, I was raised by my mom, and she worked three jobs just to keep a roof over our heads and food on the table. No one has ever ordered me a car service before and it's such a relief now.

"Not a problem at all."

I swallow down a lump. I won't ask him for hotel money for New York, I know he means if I need anything for this wedding. I briefly wonder if I should give dating another try.

I've had one boyfriend in my entire life, and it was an underwhelming and somewhat humiliating experience. But it would be nice to have someone look out for me now and then. "I'm really happy for you and Charlotte."

Leo has been silent next to his brother, his dark brown eyes assessing me. My skin goose pimples as I turn to meet his gaze again, our eyes connecting, the dark brown of his seeming to see right through me.

Did I call the Kincaids dangerous? Leo's eyes alone are downright lethal, and my gaze drops again as I nip at my lip. I've never had a reaction like this to a man and I'm not quite sure what to do with it.

"Morning, gorgeous," he says with a one-sided grin that makes my stomach do somersaults.

He's got this stubble that's not quite a shadow but it's not a beard either and it only highlights the fullness of his mouth and the square jaw that makes him look all man. His hair is a bit mussed, but somehow, it only adds to his appeal, like he just got out of bed...

I clear my throat. "Good morning."

Mason scowls at Leo before he turns back to me. "Your dress should be delivered in the next half hour. I took the liberty of choosing a pale green that will complement your hair and eyes."

I don't even ask how he might have gotten the size correct. Something tells me it will fit perfectly. "I'm sure it's lovely. Thank you again, Mason."

Leo's smile grows and I shift in the doorway.

"Mason? Is that you?" I hear Charlotte call from behind me.

I look back to see her rising from the bed. "You're not supposed to see him," I say, closing the door a little tighter around my body to block the view.

"I won't," Charlotte says as she wraps a robe about her body, the same white hotel one I'm wearing. The difference is she has a high-end negligee under hers and I've got a ratty T-shirt under mine. "I just want to talk to him through a crack in the door."

I've no choice but to step out into the hall, my bare feet on full display. At least Mason had sent a manicurist to do our fingers and toes last night. Mine have a fresh coat of pale pink polish on them that should go nicely with the dress. I curl them into the carpet as Leo gives me a long look up and down, the sort that makes my skin heat. "I don't know if you remember, but we've met before this weekend."

I shake my head. I don't really, and I feel like I would. He's not the kind of man a girl forgets.

I know the story. Charlotte went on a couple of dates with Leo a few years back and that's how she met Mason.

Leo came into the bar on a night we were both working. Case in point, he asked Charlotte out that night and not me. I don't make an impression on rich and successful guys. Not like she does.

Then again, I was probably hustling like nobody's business the night he came in.

I have a full scholarship to UNLV so I don't have to pay tuition, but the rest of my life, including all the costs of training as a dancer, I've had to finance on my own and tips is the way I make it happen.

My mom has nothing to spare to help me and I never ask. She's got her own burdens without taking on mine.

"Sort of…" I say as I look down the hall. Anywhere but at him.

"I remember you."

He steps closer and I can feel the heat of him, my nipples actually stiffen as I wrap the robe tighter around me again, keeping my arms between us.

What would it be like to have a man like this in my bed? My body pulses with a delicious ache at the idea of it, a feeling I try to tamp down.

I have a confession to make. I've only ever slept with one guy and he never actually made me…

I swallow down a lump. "You do?"

Next to me, Mason is whispering to Charlotte through the crack in the door, his hand pressed to the thick wood as though he'd like to break apart the wood with his bare hands just to look at Charlotte's face, but I can't attend a word he's saying. My whole body is focused on Leo.

I close my eyes, my chin titling up and to the side. Why I'm exposing my neck to a man I just called lethal, I don't know…

"I do." His hand comes to the wall behind me, the one I just realized I'm leaning against, his thumb brushing the indent of my waist. "And I have to confess, I'm disappointed you don't remember me."

There is no point in lying. Tomorrow I'll leave and then I'll likely never see Leo again. "I seriously doubt I'll forget you after today."

I feel him grin. Don't even ask me how that's possible but I do as he shifts closer. "Oh yeah…why is that?"

"You're…" I search for the right word. Hot as Hades? Tall, dark, and sinister? "Magnetic."

His hand slides down the wall, his thumb tracing my hip as his hand slides down my body. "Right back at you."

"Hello," a female voice calls from the other end of the hall. My eyes snap open. Mason and Leo's sister, Arabella, is walking toward us with an army of people behind her. "The cavalry has arrived!"

A rack of dresses is at the back of the group, along with several women carrying cases of different shapes and sizes.

We're all about to get major makeovers. Again.

This is Charlotte's life now? It's not without its appeal.

Leo pushes back and regret lances through me as I stand up straight, pasting a smile on my face.

An hour later, my long red hair has been twisted into some amazingly elaborate coif at the back. The dress is the perfect shade to highlight my green eyes, only further accentuated by the subtle shades of eyeliner and shadow.

And the mermaid style dress hugs my dancer's body like it was custom made for me, though I never gave anyone a single measurement.

And Charlotte...

She's never looked more beautiful. Draped in white, the strapless princess gown shows off her lush curves and classic beauty.

Her hair is down, one section pulled back with a comb at her right ear, and styled in loose waves that only make her cheekbones look even more classic and her large grey eyes even wider.

I sigh next to Arabella, Charlotte's other bridesmaid.

Charlotte is perfection.

A spread of food has been laid out in the room as we wait for the ceremony to begin, but I only pick at it. I'm nervous, which is odd. I don't mind being in front of people, it's part of being on stage, so I try to determine why I'm feeling so off.

And then I remember. Leo Kincaid. He's going to see me in this dress. And for once I look like I actually belong in their world.

Maybe I can pretend for one night...

Leo seemed interested.

And I'd love to know what all the fuss was about. And by fuss, I mean sex. Charlotte is discreet, she hasn't said much, but what she has shared tells me that the bedroom is steaming hot between her and Mason.

Making our way outside, we're not waiting for more than a minute before the delicate strains of a melodious violin announce it's time for us to walk down the aisle.

Grace is kind of my thing, but my gaze catches Leo's as he waits at the other end of the aisle with his brother. His gaze locks on mine and I nearly trip in my stilettos.

It takes all my concentration to focus on Mason and Charlotte as they say their vows, promise to love, honor, and cherish each other for the rest of their lives.

I can hear the happiness is Charlotte's voice, the promise in Mason's just before they seal their bond with a kiss.

It's so beautiful, I forget about the danger a man like Leo could bring into my life. He's a predator and I'm no match. But I don't care about that or my carefully crafted reasons for *not* having meaningless trysts. The list is long and very, very valid.

But after a glass of champagne, every reservation I had has disappeared as I step out onto the veranda to watch the sun set over the mountains.

It was a perfect day. One I'd like to remember when I'm back in Vegas hustling drinks at Rebels.

Or maybe, I'll be in New York preparing to be a professional dancer…

With a sigh, I look back and that's when I find Leo standing in the doorway behind me. My pulse stutters as a blush fills my cheeks. "Hello."

"The bride and groom are about to retire for the evening."

"Already?" I ask, and then my cheeks heat even more. Like I needed to ask why.

"My brother is very enamored with his bride."

I nod, determined not to make this anymore awkward. But Leo does that for me, moving so close I can feel my nipples tighten again.

Only this dress didn't really allow for a bra, the spaghetti straps and draped neckline make sure my small bit of cleavage is on full display.

Leo looks down and I see his eyes darken. He's noticed my nipples too.

"You know…" He leans close to my ear. "I've got a beautiful view of the rising moon from my room and tonight, it's full."

My pulse rushes in my ears as I nip at my lip. Do I actually dare to do this? Wetting my lips, I force myself to meet his gaze. He's even more handsome in his tux than he was in his T-shirt this morning.

What's more, the promise I see in his eyes has me gasping for breath.

Yeah. I think I dare…

CHAPTER TWO

Kim

My moment of internal bravery is quickly doused as Leo moves closer.

This is Charlotte's brother-in-law.

And I am no player.

Lots of men mistake me for one, it's pretty common. Between my flaming hair and something about the tilt of my green eyes, I think I give off a sex kitten kind of look but I'm not.

My mother kept me buttoned down pretty tight. Didn't want me to repeat her mistake of getting pregnant young and raising a baby alone.

While we didn't have any extra money, my mom had been a dancer too and she'd opened a small studio in town. She taught nearly every night, and I would be with her until I was old enough to stay home alone, but even then, I'd be at the studio most nights.

I loved that place. I even became a teacher there, helping some of the small girls to learn the basics. It was some of my favorite time in my whole life.

We were always moving from crappy rental to crappy rental, but that little studio had felt like home.

But those lessons she taught me about not letting men distract me, of chasing my dreams, not men, run deep. Something I try to remember as Leo leans next to me on the rail and everything about this man tells me he's way out of my league.

From his natural swagger, to his ridiculous good looks, to his money, I can't believe he'd even be interested in a single night with me. And I shouldn't want one with him.

The wedding only had about twenty guests. I'm guessing his options are just limited…

"So…" He quirks a brow. "How about it?"

My jaw drops at his open and direct invitation. Not many men can get away with that kind of ask, but somehow, he does.

I can't deny that part of me is still tempted. Attractive men proposition me often but not like Leo. There is something so supremely confident about him that makes him so appealing.

He's not faking, he just is an alpha, and that kind of energy is heady.

"Viewing the moon?" I ask, turning my back to him and looking out over the manicured lawn to the mountain beyond. From the top of the largest peak, the moon appears, a sliver that shoots rays of silver into the sky. I point my finger, "I think we can watch it from here."

He glances back over my shoulder and quirks a half grin, one side of his mouth tipping up in the sexiest way.

It's so hot, it makes my stomach flutter and an ache start between my legs. Turning my back to him to face the moon, I try to keep my breath calm.

"So we can." He says this quietly, not like he's disappointed but more like he appreciates the exchange. The challenge. Alpha. "Can I get you a drink?"

"No, thank you," I answer automatically, before I realize I'm being difficult. Looking back at him, I blush. "I have to get up at about three in the morning to make my flight to New York."

"New York?"

I nod. "I've got an audition for the New York City Ballet."

His eyes slide over me. "Dancer? I'm not surprised, you move like a dancer."

I nod again, as I hold up my empty glass. "I shouldn't have had this one, but I couldn't resist toasting to Mason and Charlotte."

He reaches for the glass, his fingers brushing mine as he takes the crystal out of my hand, setting the glass to the side. "There marriage will be a happy one, I'm sure of it."

"I hope so," I answer with a sigh. "Charlotte deserves a happy life."

"She does," Leo answers quietly in a way that has me wondering about their history. Between the tension with Mason and fact that Leo and Charlotte went out…but I was under the impression it wasn't serious.

"So, it's an early night for you with no drinks?" Leo asks, returning the conversation to me.

"That's right," I answer, reaching for the rail and gripping it tightly as I try to ignore the thrill of his interest. The New York City Ballet almost never invites dancers like me to audition, but one of my professors danced there and she recommended me.

It's an incredible honor, I try to focus on that, as I watch the moon slowly rise. But the truth is, if I don't get accepted, I have no idea what I'm going to do with my life. I need to keep focused tonight and do everything I can to make my audition a success.

His shoulder brushes mine. I hadn't even realized he was moving closer, but a shiver runs through me at the contact.

I look over at him, my eyes wide. I'm so out of my depth.

"And in terms of your audition tomorrow, do you think an orgasm would help or hurt your chances?"

My mouth goes completely dry. "Orgasm?"

He reaches out, his fingertips brushing down my spine as he leans close to my ear. "You might sleep better, be more relaxed."

"I…" I might. That's the truth. "Leo," I whisper his name. "That's a terrible idea." It's not.

"Why is that?"

"I don't know." I shake my head, trying to come up with rational arguments which completely fail me. "You're talking about a one-night thing?"

"Sure." His fingers stop at the small of my back and then his hand spreads out, his palm pressing to that spot just above my derriere. It's so intimate that I feel my breath hitch.

"I don't really do that kind of thing."

"Me either," he gives me a wicked grin. The kind that makes my cheeks heat.

"Liar."

He gives a soft laugh. "Truth? I'm turning over a new leaf." In his other hand is his own glass and he raises it giving a shake. "Water."

I reach out, this time, taking the glass from him. He lets me have it, our fingers brush again as a tingle spreads through my hand. I bring the glass to my lips, take a sip of ice-cold water. I'd hoped it would cool my heating skin, but even drinking from the same glass feels intimate as I hand the drink back to him.

"So, part of your new leaf is to offer to give a woman you just met an orgasm?"

He leans close again, and then his lips actually press to my skin. He grazes the sensitive spot at the corner of my jaw, just below my ear. I tremble with the little thrill of pleasure that courses down on me. "Yup. Definitely."

I lean back to meet his gaze. "You're serious?"

"I'm far more interested in watching you cum then I am in my own orgasm. For me, that's real progress."

I gasp, a flood of wetness soaking my thong. Never having achieved one that I hadn't given myself, it takes everything in me not to agree with his proposal. "We can't."

"Why not?"

"Because..." I lick my lips, but his gaze catches the movement of my tongue, his eyes fixing on the pink tip. I quickly draw it back in my mouth. "You're Charlotte's brother-in-law." I raise my hands in front of me like I'm creating some barrier. "What if we both get invited to Thanksgiving or something?"

"I don't really do holidays and chances are high I won't be at the next several." There is a change in his voice. Gone is the teasing confidence and in its place is something hard and unyielding.

"What?" I ask, confusion making me look back over my shoulder at him.

He shakes his head, his smile reappearing again. "I'll make you a deal. I won't be weird, if you won't."

That actually does sound reasonable or I may be trying to rationalize because I'd really like to know how it would feel to have a man like Leo touch me.

I draw in a steadying breath of air, my defenses are being stripped one by one in a way that's making me feel dizzy. "Listen," I whisper. "I don't really do this, you know? I've had like one boyfriend and—"

"Did he make you feel good?"

I blink several rapid flutters of my eyelashes. How did he know that the sex had been terrible? Do I have a sexually repressed tattooed somewhere I'm unaware of? "He…I…I don't…"

"I'll make you a second deal." His hand moves to my far hip, grasping hold, he pulls me close to his body. I'm putty in his hands and I know I'm losing.

I can feel the hard press of his erection in my other hip, but it doesn't scare me. If anything, I'm getting hotter, wetter.

I bet he'd feel so good. And he knows I'm weakening as I mold to the hard edges of his body. "What deal?" I shouldn't have asked but I can't help myself. I squeeze my thighs together, trying to relieve the ache.

"I'm going to pull you into the shadows over there where no one can see us." He points to a dark secluded corner of the veranda. "Then I'm going to push your dress up to your waist."

My pulse is thrumming through my veins, blood rushing in my ears…

"I'll drop to my knees."

Dear lord above, that sounds amazing.

"And then I'm going to eat you out until you cum all over my tongue."

"I don't..." My voice cracks on the second word.

"Five minutes, princess. If you haven't screamed my name as you break apart in less than five minutes, I'll slink off to my room and we'll avoid all eye contact at Thanksgiving."

I'm staring at him, but no words are coming out of my mouth. Because, to be completely honest, screaming his name sounds absolutely amazing.

I try to remember all the reasons this is a bad idea but I'm struggling to come up with a single one. "I have to go to bed early."

He bends down, wrapping his arm under my backside and lifts me up in the air so that I'm pressed all down his front. My response is to wrap my arms about the powerful cords of his neck.

He looks up at me since my face is now above his. "Leo." His name rolls of my tongue, and he grins again.

"Next time, I'm gonna need you to say my name a lot louder." And then his other hand slides up my back, tangling in my hair and bringing my mouth to his.

It's not a warmup kiss. Not soft and sweet. A moment after our lips meet, he parts mine, his tongue pushing into my mouth and sliding across mine. It's everything he is, aggressive, confident, hot as hell. I moan, but he swallows down the sound as he keeps kissing me, his tongue, lips, and teeth, devouring me in a way that's got me gasping for air and drowning in lust.

He sets me down on my feet without breaking the kiss. I've never made out like this before. It's the stuff of dreams, and I swear, it might be possible to orgasm from his kiss alone.

I'm throbbing with need, my panties now completely soaked through. Can he smell how excited I am?

I'm guessing yes, because he backs me up against a wall, even as his hands gather the fabric of my skirt, pulling it up my legs until it's all pooled at my waist Just like he promised.

"Not a lot of time to mess around," he whispers against my lips before he pushes one spaghetti strap off my shoulder the fabric of the dress barely being held up by my nipple.

He doesn't waste any time running his hand up my side and

cupping my breast. I'm built like a ballerina, which means I don't have the biggest chest. But they're high and tight.

He thumbs my nipple and then pushes the fabric down lower, exposing my already tight nipple to the cool night air.

"Fuck me, your tits are perfect," he says a moment before he drops his head to suck the puckered flesh into his mouth.

I cry out, loud and long, not able to hold the sound in, his mouth just feels too good.

In answer, he does the same to the other, a half sob falling from my lips. I had no idea sex could be like this. I can't think, can't breathe, and every nerve ending is waiting for is next touch. I want more.

Leo must understand what I'm thinking because he only laps at my breast for another few seconds before he drops, as promised, to his knees.

He looks up at me, a bit of moonlight catching his dark eyes and making them shine.

He looks stunningly gorgeous and completely devilish all at the same time. How can a man look that powerful down on his knees?

If this is hell...sign me up.

CHAPTER THREE

KIM

I'M LOOKING DOWN at him too, my chest rising and falling with such rapid beats, all I can hear is my breath.

The top of my dress is down, my skirt is up. I look like a woman who is about to be ravaged. Or maybe, I just look like the girl I've spent my whole life trying not to be…easy.

But I banish the thought, focusing on the man instead and the way he's making me feel.

Leo's holding me by the hips, my dress about my waist. "You smell amazing," he murmurs a second before he tips forward, nosing my mound that's still covered in my drenched panties.

I'm so turned on that even the light brush of the tip of his nose makes me throw my head back, my hips arching into him. Did he say five minutes?

I don't think I'm even going to last one.

It's so much more than I ever imagined, and I can't get enough of him.

He flattens his tongue along my thong, licking up the cloth covering my seam.

My knees buckle as I let out a gasping sob. "So good."

He chuckles with his mouth still pressed to my sex so that I actually feel the vibration of his laugh moving through me.

It only makes me hotter.

"Don't you cum yet," Leo growls into my sex. "I want my full five."

I squeeze my eyes shut and open them, attempting to clear the haze of lust. I'm trying to think, trying to calm myself down. "I'll give you more than that if you just make me…" My head thrashes back and forth as I arch my hips closer to him.

He looks up at me again, his eyes so dark and intense they steal my breath. "You want to cum, gorgeous?"

"Yes," comes my keening cry as I bury my fingers in his hair. I try to pull him closer, but he resists, still looking up at me.

"Ask nicely."

I blink down at him, desperate for what he can give me. "W-what?"

"Say please, sweetheart, and I'll give you whatever you want…"

There is no room to be self-conscious here. "Please, Leo. Please. I need it." I tighten my fingers in the silky strands, my nails digging into his scalp, even as he lifts one of my knees and settles it in on his massive shoulder.

Then he slides his index finger into my panties, brushing the lips in a way that makes me moan and buck.

But he doesn't keep rubbing me, though. Instead, he yanks the thong to the side and flattens his tongue on my clit.

I'm cumming before he's even completed a single lick, my body wound so tight that a massive shudder rocks me as I do exactly what he'd said I do, I scream his name.

But the orgasm has hardly begun before he's surging up my body.

I let out a cry of protest, wanting to ride that wave longer. No orgasm has ever felt like that one and I'm desperate to eke out every last ounce of pleasure.

"One second, gorgeous, and I'm going to make you feel even

better. Promise." He yanks at his own trousers, ripping them open and shoving then down his hips.

I watch transfixed. Even with his shirt still on and partially covering his dick, my mouth falls open. "Holy shit." I never swear. But I can't hold it in. He's so big, I'm staring at his erection with my eyes about to fall out of my head.

He's hooking my knee again, closing the distance between us as he places my leg around his waist. "Never seen a big dick before?"

"No," I answer honestly. "I haven't."

My words make him pause, the mushroom head pressed to my vagina. I've got to be honest, it feels good. So good.

He's got one arm around my back and the other hand cradles my skull, his fingers splaying up into my hair. My updo has got to be in tatters, half undone, but I can't bring myself to care. "You're good to do this?" he asks, not moving for a moment as he stares down at me, holding my gaze.

Am I good to feel even better? "I'm good."

It's all he needs to start pushing inside me. He feels so good but also…I wince a little and stiffen.

"Jesus, Kim, you're tight."

"Yeah. I…"

"You're not a virgin, are you?"

"No," I shake my head. "But I don't have much experience. I…" I don't want to talk about anyone but him. It feels wrong. So instead, I try to relax. "I know this whole night, us, has been super fast. But I just need a little slow for a minute."

He cradles me even closer as he stills his hips again, pushing into me in small increments that allow me to adjust.

I try to marry these two men in my mind, the super confident alpha and the man who asks permission, who delays his needs for mine, and who takes the time to make it good for me. But maybe a guy who is really confident is best able to care for my needs. I can't think on it now…

When he's almost all the way inside of me, he hits some spot that doesn't hurt at all. In fact, "Leo," I gasp, digging my nails into his neck. "Oh God, that…"

He tightens his hold on me, pressing even deeper and making me vibrate with need. Then he pulls out and pushes back in.

There is no pain this time and the pleasure starts much earlier in the thrust, the way he rubs my insides, making me so full, I can't even think a coherent thought as I hang onto to his muscled shoulders.

He picks up the pace, thrusting in and out of me moving faster and faster as my body matches his rhythm.

I may not have experience, but I do have a few assets. Namely, my stamina and my athleticism and I use them both now as I tighten my leg around his waist and use the grip on his torso to swing the other one up and around his waist too so that I'm completely off the ground and being supported by his hands and the circle of my legs.

It makes him sink even deeper into me, and I give a long keening moan at how good it feels to be that full.

He's grunting in my ear, as he nips at my lobe. "You feel so fucking good, Kim."

"So do you." My head tilts to the side to give him even more access to my neck. He bottoms out inside me again, the press of his pelvis as he buries himself deep, making my clit throb.

I know this is a one-time deal. I get it. Which is why I try to hold out. I want to feel this for as long as possible.

Because the way he's pounding me, I never want him to stop. "Leo." My voice is broken and breathy as I pull at his hair. "I'm trying not to cum, it's so good, I want it to last, but I can't…"

"Fuck, princess," he's growling in my ear. "Cum all over my cock. Soak me."

The words break the final band of control that I'd had and screaming his name, I do exactly what he told me to do. I cum like I've never cum before, the orgasm so powerful, stars appear behind my lids as my entire body spasms, every muscle joining in.

It's his cue, and with a roar, he joins me. He hammers in and out of me, pumping me full as he holds me tight.

I feel him slow even as he convulses with his orgasm, but his arms are still locked around me, supporting my weight.

Which is fine by me, I don't want to leave his arms yet. I didn't think about this part. The part where we have to disengage and then what...shake hands?

Say some awkward goodbye?

I have this weak moment where I want to ask...can we see each other again? But Leo Kincaid is a king of Vegas and I'm still just a wannabe dancer who grew up on this side of the poverty line.

This was a one-time thing and, if I've got one thing, it's pride. Besides, I'm leaving for New York, hopefully for good and he'll be in Vegas. There was never a future.

I must stiffen with my thoughts because he eases back. "That was..."

I nip at my lip, my insecurity making my throat tight. "Don't tell me it was average."

"It wasn't."

"Good," I whisper, with a shake of my head, my hair falling down my back. We're up against the wood of the natural siding and I'm going to guess it ruined my designer dress too. I wince as I think about what type of girl lets a man she barely knows do her on the side of a building, ruining her nice clothes and hair. "Because I've never experienced anything like it."

He leans in and captures my lips, giving me a long slow kiss that makes me soften again, makes the worries disappear. Is it weird to thank him for making this less awkward with a bit of tenderness?

Then again, it's clear that Leo is a man who knows what he's doing. That's why I did this with him in the first place.

"After New York, are you coming back to Vegas?"

I nod. "I have a class to finish up, a final to take so I can graduate this summer..." And then who knows. I certainly don't. But I've got my hopes.

"And after that?"

"With any luck, I'll be moving to New York."

"New York? That's far..."

I give a small nod. "That's the idea."

He gives me a long stare…one that makes the hair on the back of my neck stand up again. "Is it? Leaving Vegas is the goal?"

"Being a ballet dancer is the goal."

His thumb is stroking over my cheek. "But you'll be in Vegas for a week? A month before you leave?"

I shake my head. "My last final is in two days. The moment it's done, I can leave for New York if the ballet wants me."

"Hmmm." I can hear some disapproval in his tone, and I cock my head, attempting to figure it out.

His hand slides over my butt, giving it a squeeze before he kisses me again. "But we were just getting to know each other." It's strange. My top is still down, my legs around his waist, but some odd fear has made my pulse hitch. His voice is laced with the danger I can always feel just under the surface with him.

"You don't mean that," I shake my head, untangling my arms and pulling as far back as I can with the wall behind me. "I know what this is."

"What is it?"

"A one-time thing. A wedding hook-up." I look at him but we're in the shadows and his eyes are dark and unreadable.

"Call me when you get back. Let me know how the audition goes?"

It wasn't what we agreed. I know that. Just like I know I'm one girl in a long line of them. But maybe this is his way of making goodbye easier? "Sure."

Slowly, we untangle and he's gentleman enough to straighten my gown pulling down the skirt of my dress and sliding my little spaghetti straps back up my arms. The last is done with a soft kiss that has me forgetting the weirdness before.

Then, he grabs my matching pale green clutch from where I left it on the rail and hands it to me.

I swallow down a lump, not sure what to say. "That was really great," I whisper, feeling the awkwardness color my cheeks.

"It was better than great." He walks me to my room, his hand strong and sure on the small of my back. Boy, does he know how to do a one-night stand right, giving me one more slow kiss goodbye. It's enough to make it easier to part ways, close the door. I'm not calling, he doesn't want me to.

This was not some beginning. This was a beautiful mistake, one I'll likely spend years feeling bad about.

When I'm not secretly dreaming about Leo Kincaid's touch.

CHAPTER FOUR

Kim

My foot taps with impatience as I watch the flight board at LaGuardia Airport. My flight has been delayed…again.

It's a terrible ending to a terrible day.

Or has it been two days? It feels like a lifetime ago since Leo had me pressed against that wall, though I'm still sore between the legs.

I'd gone back to my room and put myself back together for bed, realizing that he'd never given me his number. It really had all been a line. Nothing more.

Fine. It was better.

We'd agreed it was a single night. But I hadn't been able to sleep. I'd barely managed a few hours before I had to get up and take the car to the airport.

The flight had been hellishly long, and the traffic in New York worse.

I'd barely arrived in time for my four o'clock call time, though it hadn't mattered. Dozens of dancers had yet to be seen and the tryouts had begun at eight in the morning. There must have been a hundred dancers at the audition, at least. All of them, the best of the best.

This was their open call and everyone who had dreams of being a professional ballet dancer was there.

I finally was seen at seven, and I could say this. I'd given my absolute best.

Not that the panel judging me had even cracked a smile. They hadn't. I'd just gotten the stock response, *you'll hear from us in a week or two*. And then I was sent on my way.

I took a cab back to the airport, where I'd sort of slept on a row of chairs. Like I mentioned, no hotel money. And after two nights of barely sleeping, I'd woke to find that my seven o'clock flight back to Vegas was delayed. Which was a major problem.

I had a final this afternoon. It was my last class I'd taken during the summer session, and I needed to pass to get my degree.

Furiously, I typed an email to my professor on my phone, thanking my lucky stars that I had enough charge to send it.

Then, I sidled up to the desk.

"May I help you?" The attendant gives me a thin smile that tells me she is nearly out of patience.

I'm sure I'm not the first person to ask what's going on with our flight. "Any word on when we'll board?"

The smile grows more brittle. "Hopefully in the next half hour, but maybe longer, depending."

"Depending? What's wrong?"

"Mechanical issues."

I sigh, I can't wait much longer. "Any other flights I can take? I really need to get home."

She looks down at her screen, tapping away. "Delta has one leaving in fifteen minutes. If you hurry..."

"Oh, that would be great!" I say, relief rushing through me. Professor Stilton, my Latin teacher, is a stickler for the rules. I'd put off taking the required language courses, a choice I now regret.

Because if I missed this final, there was no way she'd pass me.

"Let me book it for you," she taps away. "The additional fee will be six hundred fifty-two dollars and twenty-three cents."

My jaw drops. It was twice the price of the original flight. "Oh."

She looks up at me, understanding why I haven't just pulled out my credit card. "Or you can wait for this one."

I nod, my shoulders slumping. I don't have $653. Not in my checking or savings. I don't even have it in credit. Once a month, something comes up I can't pay for, and it goes on the plastic.

My shoulders slumping, I return to my seat. Firing up my phone, I see an email from Stilton.

Clicking it open, I get through the first seven words: *I'm sorry, but there are no exceptions...*before my phone dies.

"Great," I mutter, my eyes sliding closed. Today is not my day.

The flight finally boards two hours later and I know I have no hope of making the final. It means I'll fail the class.

Which means I'll have to pay out of pocket to take it again next semester. That's if I'm not leaving for New York.

The idea of leaving Vegas without my degree makes me wince.

Some guy takes the seat next to me. He's good looking and athletic, and I can see by the way his gaze keeps sliding to mine that he's interested.

I've never been less so.

Between my irritation and what happened with Leo, I can't even imagine flirting with this guy, or any guy really.

"Going to Vegas?"

I look over at him, my brows drawn together. Is he serious? We're all sitting in the same airplane. "Yep."

"Me too. Can't wait. I've never been."

I shake my head. If he's looking for a vacation hook up, he can forget it. "Have fun."

"You on vacation too?"

I try not to sigh. "No. I go to school there."

He's blond and tan with decent muscles. I'm sure some girl would love his attention. "Oh, cool. That must be great. I go to Harvard, which is super intense. I sometimes wish I'd gone somewhere less serious."

Did he just insult me while agreeing with me? "Yeah. Sure," I'm already done talking to him, so I start searching for a plug for my charger. I need to finish reading that email. Maybe Stilton threw me some Hail Mary and there is something I can do to pass her class.

"You..." He gives me a wavering smile like he's working up the confidence to ask. Such a turn off. "You wouldn't be free tomorrow night, would you?"

I stop searching, my brain going to back to Leo's proposition. The one where he promised me an orgasm via his tongue in five minutes or less. That was the offer of a king. This one... "Sorry. No."

His smile falls. "Sure. I understand."

Mentally, I wonder what he understands. I didn't offer an explanation, but I go back to searching for a plug. I'm not trying to hurt this guy's feelings, I just have actual problems I'm trying to solve.

Finally, I find one and plug in my phone cord, waiting with bated breath. But nothing happens. The phone doesn't charge.

"Crap," I mutter under my breath as I let out a long sigh.

"Phone issues?" he asks.

Is he still here? "Just a dead battery."

He sets down his bag and starts rifling through, pulling out some slick black thing or other. "Portable charger." And then he hands it to me.

Finally, something is going right. "Thank you," I gush on a breath of air. "I'm about to miss a final and I was reading the email from my professor when my phone died." I plug in the battery and the phone instantly comes to life.

"Hot mess?" he asks, and my chin snaps up. Did he really just ask me that? But I don't answer as my email pops back up on the screen.

I'd had this one class to take during the summer semester and then I would be done. Technically, I already walked for graduation, but I don't have my degree yet.

Stilton's email comes up and I wilt again. Either I show up for the final or I fail. I should have known.

I knew I was cutting it close but…

I can feel tears welling in my eyes as my elbow drops to my knee and my head falls onto my hand.

This is bad. Really bad.

I know the course will cost a minimum of five thousand to retake and its money I don't have.

"So…what about that date?"

"What?" I lift my head back up as I look at the guy next to me.

"Tomorrow?" his gaze slides down me. "I've kind of got a thing for hot messes."

My mouth opens and then closes a moment before I unplug his charger and hand it back to him. "Have fun in Vegas."

It takes another hour before we finally taxi out to the runway and take off. On the bright side, I've got plenty of time to figure out how I'm going to retake that class. I finally get my charger to work.

But as my phone recharges, another email comes up, this one from the Ballet Company.

They want to thank me for auditioning, but they don't currently have a spot for me. They'll let me know if anything changes.

I don't cry. The Harvard dick is sitting in the same row as me and I won't give him the satisfaction of confirming that I am a hot mess.

On the bright side, I get to work my ass off to make enough money to retake Stilton's class.

But I don't see how this day could get any worse.

Then again, the universe can be a real jerk sometimes.

CHAPTER FIVE

LEO

ONE MONTH LATER...

THE GIRL in front of me twerks her hips, giving me her best come-hither stare and I try not to curl my lip. I don't want to say the only emotion I feel is disgust but...

These women are all the same.

Bottle blondes with fake tits and even faker smiles. Don't even get me started on the fake orgasms. I've slept with my fair share of them over the years.

Even before I took over the management of all the nightclubs for Kincaid Enterprises, I was around our clubs a lot.

In all, we own ten of them, but Temptation is our largest and most successful. So I am forever hiring new cage dancers to fill out our roster.

They bring in the crowds, which is why I pay them ridiculous amounts of money. But I also keep super stringent rules. No drinking, no drugs, and no hooking up at the club.

And that means, seventy percent of the girls wash out within a month.

I rake a hand through my hair as I make a note on my clipboard. I've got to be honest, I hate being a clipboard guy.

My father was a straight-up gangster, working for the Italian mafia until they killed him for sleeping with the boss's wife.

That's when Mason took over all Kincaid business. He's made us legit and made the family billionaires. But some part of me was meant to be holding a pistol, not a flimsy piece of wood with a stupid metal clip.

Then again, following in his footsteps as a gangster likely means an untimely death and I'm trying to avoid that, but somehow, I seem to make a lot of the same decisions he did, which really pisses me off.

"Next," I call as the girl stops dancing, scowling at me.

"Fuck you," she spits before she turns on her heel and stomps off, picking a wedgy out of her ass from her too-tight dance leotard.

"Classy," I mutter.

My uncle Jake, who is only a few years older than I am, turns his head, cracking his neck as he scoffs my way. "Since when do you care about class?"

I don't answer. "Next," I yell again.

Jake gives me a light push on the shoulder. "The only reason I'm here is to find a fresh piece of ass. You're harshing the experience."

I turn to glare at him. "We both know you're here to keep an eye on me, which I don't appreciate. And find your next hook-up at one of the casinos. The dancers aren't supposed to be fucking anyone while they're working. And family members are a definite no."

"Hey," Jake holds up his hands, his dark Kincaid hair pushed back from the strong features of his face. "I'm doing you a favor. If they break the rules with me now, you don't have to process the paperwork later."

I let out a grunt. "You're a human resource nightmare." To be clear,

I don't give a shit about any of that, but Jake is irritating me. I'm beginning to loathe this part of the job and he's not helping.

He's been around all the time lately, and I know why. My family is keeping tabs on me. Granted, they've got good reasons. I'm not exactly known for keeping my head and I've got a few ideas that might really piss some people off in Vegas. What my family sometimes fails to understand is that they need me stirring the pot to get rid of the shit that's settled to the bottom of our world.

"And you've got a stick up your ass."

The next girl enters from off the dressing room just as the main door swings open, my brother Roman striding into the room from the back at the same time.

Roman is a mini-Mason, polished, calculating, and if he's here, I probably did something wrong. Do they know I've been spying on Toni Carcetti, watching his movements to learn his schedule, find his weakness?

I curse under my breath as my brother slides into the seat next to me.

But I ignore him as I turn to the next dancer. "Name?"

"Chandra," she says with a smile that actually doesn't set my teeth on edge. She's blonde but it's natural, which I like. She's tall and statuesque. I already know I'll hire her.

"What are you dancing to today, Chandra?"

She's got a leotard on and nothing else. "Rihanna. 'Only Girl.'"

I give her a nod and the music starts. She's graceful, pretty. Not sexy like the dancers I usually use for the cages. I'm still hiring her, though. There are floor dancers who also carry drinks and she'd be perfect for that.

"Not bad," Jake mutters.

"Don't even fucking think it," I reply through gritted teeth. "I'd like to hire this one. Fuck the last one."

"The wedgy girl?" Jake asks, with a shake of his head. "No thanks."

Roman suppresses a smile on the other side of me. "Club life treating you well?"

"Fine." If Roman wants to be coy, I'll play along. "But can you take Jake to one of your casinos to find pussy? He's sniffing around and it's irritating me."

"Don't listen to him," Jake waves his hand as Chandra keeps dancing. "If one of us needs to get laid, it's Leo. His foul mood the last few weeks has been epic."

I snarl at him, knowing he's right. The longer Kim goes without calling, the pissier I get. With what I've got planned, my time here in Vegas is limited and I don't want to spend it waiting around for her to get over being shy. That woman felt way too good.

Besides, I jumped through several hoops to make sure she came back to Vegas, and it would really irritate me if it was all for naught.

My conscience tickles in the back of my neck, telling me that what I did to Kim was wrong. I shouldn't have messed with her life. But that was the best fucking sex of my life and I'd like to hit that a few more times. Selfish? Yes.

I told her I was turning over a new leaf, and I'm trying, but everyone knows I'm still a work in progress. And with what I've got planned, I deserve a little bit of sweet to help wash down the sour.

Why hasn't she called?

Like I already mentioned, I've been with my share of dancers, but no woman has ever ridden me like that. I want her again and the longer I go, the more irritable I get.

I could call Charlotte, get Kim's number. But then I'd have to deal with Mason and the questions he'd inevitably ask about why I wanted Charlotte's best friend's number.

My brother and I called a temporary truce for his wedding, but things have been rough between us, mostly my fault as usual, and so I'm giving him space. And trying, for once in my life, to not piss him off. It's a struggle.

Which probably means I shouldn't have fucked his wife's best friend. But I've never been good at staying out of trouble.

And that is the real reason Jake is next to me. I stirred the pot a few months back with some of our rivals and we're still dealing with the fallout. Coincidentally, that is the exact reason I should have kept it in my pants at Mason's wedding.

And while I'm trying to be better, I think it might be clear, I'm just a fuck up. So, my new plan. Fuck something up that actually helps my family and only hurts me. Might mean prison. Might mean I end up dead in a gutter.

See? This is why I deserve another hit of Kim before it's too late.

"Didn't he just get laid?" Roman asks, sitting back in his chair, his knees spread wide in a casual masculine stance that makes Chandra miss a step as her eyes lock on him.

Fuck. I hope I can still hire her.

But Roman looks at me, barely noticing the dancer and Chandra falls back into step.

"Yeah, he did," Jake chuckles. "You'd think he'd be in a good mood after that one."

"What are you talking about?" I grit the words through clenched teeth, not liking the two of them clucking around me like fucking mother hens.

Both of them laugh, though, neither of them concerned by the warning in my voice. I might be an alpha but they both match me in their own ways. "I'm not sure who she was, but whoever you managed to corner at Mason's wedding was a screamer." Jake pulls out a cigar, running the fat roll under his nose.

"I've got be honest, big brother," Roman shakes his head. "I wouldn't mind getting my hands on a woman who sounds like that. It was fucking hot."

"Both of you need to shut up," I spit. Which should be one of many indicators that something isn't right. Normally, I'd want to revel in the moment of a good lay with them. But for some reason, it makes me furious that they heard Kim. That they know this about her. Those screams were for me and me alone.

Then again, I am the one who fucked her right outside the open doors of a wedding reception. I should have taken her to my room. If she hadn't been so skittish, I would have. But I'd like to have trapped her in my bed for a lot longer.

Because I swear, the more time that passes, the more I want her. It's taking over my waking brain and soon, I'm going to have to grovel to Charlotte and then deal with Mason. He broke my nose the last fight, not that I care.

But still, I hate it when his anger is justified and lately, it has been. I wonder what he'd think of what I did to Kim. Or what I'm about to do to Toni Carcetti.

The music dies and Chandra stops dancing.

I ignore both Roman and Jake, giving her a tight jerk of my chin. "That was great."

"Really?" she gives me a genuine smile, her hands clasping in front of her. "I'm so glad."

"When can you start?"

Her smile grows. "Whenever."

I check her off on my clipboard. "Check in with Melissa and she'll get the paperwork going. I'm going to start you on the floor and…" I see her smile slip a bit before she pastes it back on. She knows the cage dancers make the most money.

"That's great. Thank you."

I've only got a few names left and I haven't hired a new cage dancer yet. I could bump Chandra into the roll, but I know she's not the best dancer for the position. "Chandra, you have any friends looking for a gig?"

She shifts. "I might. My roommates are all dancers and I know Kim really needs money so—" She stops, maybe worried she's revealing too much.

But I straighten. I'm sure there are a thousand dancers named Kim in this city, but a fission of energy runs down my limbs. "Kim? What kind of dancer is Kim traditionally?"

"Ballet. She had this killer interview in New York but…" Chandra stops again.

But I barely can contain my string of curses. How many Kims, who are dancers, just went to interview in New York? "And she needs money?"

Chandra nods. "I mean, I don't want to speak for her cause she's got all kinds of rules about what she will and won't do dance wise and dating wise too, but I can tell her you're hiring if you want."

I need to be sure we're talking about the same person. "I want someone with striking looks."

"Oh, that's Kim, for sure. Long red hair, tall, gorgeous."

That's my girl. My fingers flex with anticipation as I grip the clipboard, but I try to hide the tell from Roman and Jake.

I don't want them to know about this plan or any other I'm making.

They're both looking at me, but I don't glance at either of them. "She's exactly what I'm searching for. Tell her if she comes in tomorrow or Friday, I'll pay her double."

Chandra starts in surprise and then frowns, and I realize my mistake. "Same for you, Chandra. If you bring me some more dancers, I'll give you a generous finder's fee."

She perks back up, nodding enthusiastically.

I sit back, my bad mood evaporating. I might have found my Kim without involving Mason at all.

This is perfect.

I rip a paper from my clipboard, scribbling some hours and a figure that I hope will coerce Kim into coming in to audition.

Standing up, I walk toward Chandra and if she'd noticed Roman before, now her gaze is on me, her eyes dilating in that way that I know she's interested.

I give her one of my most charming smiles, leaning close. "Thanks, Chandra. I really hope you can bring Kim in for me."

She smiles back, a flush filling her cheeks. "I bet she will. She failed that class, so I know she needs the money."

My smile slips because that ticks me off. Is she really suffering? Why hasn't she asked for help? It's so easy to pay for one class.

I clear my throat, banishing the thought, because that's not my place. At least not right at this moment. Maybe not at all. I'm not the make-a-commitment kind of guy. But there are some perks to dating a guy who's got more money than he knows what to do with.

I mean if I'm going to be the guy that ruined her New York opportunity, the least I can do is pay for some of the damage.

But I shut those thoughts down. I'll figure all that out later, right now, I just want to see her again. And I definitely want her in my bed…

CHAPTER SIX

Kim

I crack my eyes open, trying to figure out what time it is and what woke me. I've been exhausted this week and I have no idea why.

My phone rings and I realize that's what must have interrupted my sleep.

Lifting my head, the harsh shrill of the ring sounds in my ear again, and I reach out a fumbling hand, trying to swim from the fog long enough to make the sound stop.

I pick it up and see my mom's name flash across the screen. Letting out a long groan, I stare at the screen for a beat longer before I finally answer.

I know we haven't talked very much the last month…

To be honest, I'm not exactly proud of what I did with Leo. In fact, it's everything my mom has warned me my entire life not to do.

She was nineteen when she got pregnant with me, I have no idea who my dad is. He was never around, I don't even know if he knows I exist.

We've never discussed it. What I do know is that my mom has told me a thousand times if she's told me once, not to get carried away by attractive men.

To stick to my goals and to make something of myself. It's become like this mantra in my head.

"Hey Mom," I croak into the phone.

"Kimmy?" she replies back. "Are you still sleeping?"

"Umm," I answer. "Yeah."

"It's one in the afternoon."

I pull the phone away from my ear and stare at the screen. So it is. "I've been working a ton of doubles and not getting out until really late. Just a bit worn out."

I swear, I can hear her nodding. "It's really too bad about that class. I'm sorry you have to retake it for an interview that didn't even…"

"It's fine." That's the other reason I've been avoiding my mom. I think she might be as disappointed as I am about the New York Ballet. Maybe more.

It was her dream before it was mine and I know it kills her that I got so close and then didn't succeed.

She worked really hard to get me here. I hate disappointing her.

"Are you eating healthy?" she asks, going into dance mom mode, I swear. "Getting studio time?"

"Mom, I'm good." I plant my face back into my pillow.

"What about dating, sweetheart?"

"Mom." I do not want to start on this.

"You've hardly seen anyone since that nice boy, freshman year."

"I know." Chasing the dream of a professional dancer does not leave me much time for dating and the boyfriend wasn't all that nice. "I've been really busy."

MAYBE I NEED SOME COFFEE. I'm not a regular drinker but I need some fortification for this conversation. The truth is, I just gave up my studio hours because I can't afford to pay for them and my class. Once I get my degree and I can get a day job, hopefully as a choreographer or dance teacher, I can afford studio time again.

The idea of spending all day teaching actually makes me happier, and the feeling perks me up enough to push myself out of bed.

I put the phone on speaker so that I can shrug on a tank top before heading out to the kitchen.

As a group of dancers who spend a lot of time changing together, none of my roommates wear very much around the apartment so it's not weird that I'm coming out of my room in nothing but a tank and underwear.

I mute the phone as I step into the bathroom and swish out my mouth and then run a brush through my hair. My natural curls are an unruly mass this morning, but I'll straighten them after coffee.

On the other end of the phone, my mom is chattering away. Her classes are good, she's moving again.

I unmute the phone, bringing it to my ear. "Why are you moving this time?"

"My current landlord wants to take advantage of the hot market and sell," she sighs. "It would be so nice to own my own place so I don't have to move every two years."

I wince as I start for the kitchen, sure there will be some left over coffee. We all work late as waitresses or dancers, our studio time taking place in the late morning or afternoon so there is usually coffee in the pot all day.

But the soft murmur of voices makes me stop in the hall.

I hear Chandra chattering away but, some other tone catches my notice. Did I imagine it or was there a male rumble to accompany her voice?

I stop listening to my mom, focusing on the conversation in the kitchen, but I only hear Chandra. Maybe she's on the phone. Which is good. She's been pestering me to interview at some club that is not my style at all and she's being really annoying about it. Which is saying a lot. Chandra never stops talking. Not even when she's sleeping with a guy. I would know, her room is next to mine.

I have three roommates, all Las Vegas dancers, so a fair number of guys end up sleeping over here.

Danielle, a petite blonde who's a few years older than me, has a steady boyfriend, and he's had to kick out some drunk assholes more than once. He's a good guy.

But Chandra and Kendall both have terrible taste in men.

Muting the phone again, I stop just outside the kitchen, and decide I should just peek around the corner to see if more clothing is appropriate.

Sure enough, I catch a broad shoulder in my quick view, a man's back to me as he sits at our tiny kitchen table.

Leaning back over, my brow scrunches. There is something so familiar about the set of that shoulder.

"Kim?" Chandra calls. "Is that you? Are you finally up?"

"Hang on," I say, turning to go back to my room to put on a pair of shorts at least. But before I've even completed the pivot, a man stands and steps from the kitchen and I audibly gasp as a tall, dark, and devastating man catches the side of my vision.

Leo.

My chin notches up, my eyes moving from his broad chest, to his muscled arms, to those massive shoulders. They continue over the thick cords of his neck, over the square jaw, stopping at the one-sided wolfish smile he's now wearing.

"Hello, gorgeous."

"You," I gasp back, my brain still not really processing. How is Leo here?

Chandra appears next to him, looking for all the world like the cat who got the milk. Did Leo hook up with my roommate?

Something dark and ugly bottoms out in my belly and I unmute the phone. "Mom, I've got to go."

"But we just got on the phone," she complains. "I've barely talked to you all month."

"I'll call you tomorrow," I promise before I quickly hang up and then spin, starting down the hall for my tiny room before I legit start to cry.

I'm not usually emotional, but I don't really have time to think about it as I reach my door and push into my room, grabbing the handle to slam it behind me.

But a very large hand stops the swing before it can shut.

Leo pushes the door open and slides into my room, closing it behind him.

I stare at him, my mouth surely agape. This is my room…what does he think he's doing? "Get out."

One eyebrow cocks up. "Hang on, princess."

"Don't princess me," I spit back. "I am not your princess."

His eyes are moving over me now and I know he's taking in the fact that I'm braless, in a tiny tank and a little pair of bikini briefs.

I see his eyes darken as he takes a step closer.

"Leo," I hold up a hand to keep my space. "Get out of my room."

"I need to talk to you."

"Well, I don't need to talk to you."

He shakes his head, looking wary and a bit guilty. "Why are you so pissed?"

I wave my hand in the general direction of Chandra. "What are you doing here with my roommate, as if I don't know?"

Understanding dawns in his eyes, followed by a pleased little grin that makes me squirm. "You're jealous," he says, his smile growing.

"I'm totally fine with our arrangement, Thanksgiving and all that, but keep your dick out of my roommates."

"I'm a free man and I can do what I want with my dick," he says and then he takes another step toward me.

My hand drops and lands on my hip, even as my chin notches. Because two can play that game. "Does that mean I'm free to sleep with your brother Roman?"

His smile is gone in a second, his gaze so fierce, I ought to be afraid. I don't have time, because one of his arms wraps about my back, the other around my thighs as he pulls me to his chest and lifts me in the air.

I can't deny, that even as furious as I am, a part of my body still responds to him. He feels so good against me.

My hands automatically come to his shoulders to steady myself. "Only if you want me to kill my brother."

I blink down at him, sure he's joking, but he looks dead serious.

"So you're free to sleep with whomever..." And I wave toward the kitchen again.

Leo sighs, but he doesn't put me down. "I didn't touch your roommate. She's not my style."

Now I'm completely confused. He sounds like he's being honest. "Then, why are you here?"

He looks up at me, then, one of his hands slides up to cup my exposed butt cheek. His fingers curl around the flesh so that his fingertips are dangerously close to my... "You didn't call."

Now it's my turn to be confused. "Call?"

He holds me for another second before he lowers me to the ground. The moment he steps away, I miss his hands on my bare skin.

Doing a quick sweep of the room, he walks over to my tiny vanity that's covered in scarves, hats, and purses, and he pulls off the tiny pale green clutch I used at the wedding. Then he hands it to me.

Pushing open the clasp, I open it and instantly gasp. Because inside is his business card...with his number. "I didn't...that wasn't..." But clearly, in the craziness of going to New York and then coming back, I missed the fact that Leo had, in fact, given me his number.

A flush climbs up my cheeks as I try to decide how I feel about this new information. Or how much I liked his arms around me just now.

"It was and you didn't. Call."

I nip at my lip, not sure what that means. "You're here to ask me out?"

He scowls at me, his arms crossing over his large chest. "No. I'm here to offer you a job."

Is it just me or does this day just keeping getting weirder? Tossing the clutch on the bed, I pass Leo to head back to the kitchen. "I think I need coffee."

Leo follows me out of the room and into the kitchen, where I grab a mug. "Do you want some?" I ask.

"Of that? No," he answers, returning to his seat.

I grab the pot and pour out a cup, clutching it in my hands as I go to take a sip.

But it smells awful. How long ago was this made? I wrinkle my nose and set the cup down again. "Good choice. This smells rancid or something."

The kitchen is about as small as it can be while still functionable, so Leo sitting in the chair is barely two feet from where I stand at the pot. His hand shoots out, cupping my hip as he pulls me closer again.

I'm trying to keep up. Didn't he just say that he wasn't here to ask me out?

CHAPTER SEVEN

LEO

I WANT TO BE PISSED. Kim had my number this whole time and just never bothered to call.

And I just told her that I wasn't here to ask her out and yet…I can't keep my hands off her.

Her skin slides like silk under my palm as I trace her hip. It should be illegal for skin to feel this good.

"Do you want to get dressed and I'll take you out for coffee?" I hear myself say even as I pull her closer again, my other hand reaching out so I'm holding both her hips in my hands. Her body looks so small, then again, my hands have always been large. Her much paler skin glows against my darker tone.

Even now, I want to yank down those little panties and bury my face in her—

"I don't think that's a good idea."

My chin snaps up as I glare. "Why not?"

"Leo," she whispers, her hands coming to her hips to cover mine. "Because."

"Because why?" Why is this girl giving me the cold shoulder? Does she know the truth?

"Because we said it was going to be a one-time thing and I told you…" She bends down to whisper close to my ear but the tank top gapes down, giving me an amazing view of her cleavage. I seriously love her tits. Not that big but just full enough to fill my palms with the prettiest rosy-pink nipples. "I don't do that sort of thing. Like ever."

I skate my hands over her narrow waist to her ribs, wanting to cup both those perfect tits in my hands. "What sort of thing?"

I know I'm playing dumb, but I want her to explain. I need to make sure she hasn't figured out too much about me or what I did.

"Look. Before you, I've only slept with one guy and…"

I hear a gasp from the hall and realize we've got an eavesdropper. "Chandra," I bark. "Get lost."

"All right," she says in a rush of breath before I hear her door open and close again. Chandra's been a wealth of information on Kim. Kim doesn't date, she doesn't work in clubs as a dancer, and she doesn't even really go out. It's work, class, dance, repeat.

Which only makes me like her more. "So am I only the second guy you've fucked?"

"What I did with Bobby could hardly be called fucking," she replies and then shakes her head.

I get the picture. He didn't make her scream his name. Which could only mean that she really enjoyed what we did…so…what the fuck?

I'm getting tired of the circles we're talking in, so I pull her down into my lap. She only resists for a second before she folds into me, sitting sideways across my legs.

I dip my chin to kiss the spot between her collarbone and neck. "I'm not sure I'm seeing the problem."

"We shouldn't have…" she whispers but she's arching her neck to give me more access. "I'm not that girl."

A frown pulls at my mouth. I've got a few choices here. I want Kim in my bed on the regular until all my plans have come to fruition. I know that much.

Normal me would go firing off and insist we go out, but I can sense that's not the way I get Kim, and besides, I'm trying for self-improvement, even if I'm failing.

Some deep part of me is surprised I'm softening for her. It's not like me...

Then again, enough dancers have passed through my doors for me to know, no other woman is going to scratch the itch I've been working up. And Kim needs a bit of gentle convincing. Just like last time.

"Which girl are you?" I murmur into her skin.

"I'm the girl who breaks the mold. Who does more than anyone expected."

Ah. She's that girl. "I think you're spectacular."

She shakes her head. "You think what every guy thinks about me."

"Oh yeah, what's that?"

"I get that you've got a better reason to think it than most."

Now we're getting somewhere, but I'm not sure I like it. "What do I think?"

"That I'm the trashy slut who just sleeps with a guy on the veranda at a wedding." I hear the tremor and I know we're getting to the heart of it.

"We did not do any sleeping." She shivers, her shoulders curling in and closing my access to her neck. I don't like it. "I think you're the woman that I can't stop thinking about," I answer because I've closed my fair share of deals, and all girls want to be told they're special. Though, Kim actually is.

She shakes her head. "I didn't get the job in New York." Her voice trembles and I can hear how upset she is.

My stomach bottoms out in guilt. "I heard."

"And I failed my class."

"I heard that too."

Her arms are wrapping around me like she's been drowning and I've come to rescue her. For whatever reason, that doesn't annoy me. In fact, I hold her tighter. Fuck. I'm such an asshole. "My scholarship has run out and I have to pay to retake the class out of pocket and..."

She's close to tears. I know she was just talking to her mom, but my guess is mom either doesn't know or can't pay. "You need money."

She jerks back. "I'm not asking you—"

"I need a dancer," I say levelly. I'm not promising Kim to be her doting boyfriend. I don't think she'd take the offer if I did.

But five minutes with her and she's been against my body, in my lap. If I get her in my club every day, I'm sure I can get her back in my bed.

Kim still wants me, it's completely clear.

Even now, I skate my hand up her ribs, my thumb settling just under her tit and her nipple puckers, pointing out through the tank top.

I want to bend down and suck her into my mouth so badly, my cock is at full attention in my jeans.

She looks at me, her gaze level with mine and she nips at her lip like she can't decide. "I don't do gigs like that."

I study her for a second, ticking back through several of the things she shared. I'm one of two guys she's slept with.

There's a mom, no mention of a dad, and no money.

She said I thought about her what all guys think...

Is that what she thinks about herself? I've met a lot of women in my time and Kim, despite our hook up, is as far from trashy as a woman can be.

She's all class and it shows in everything she does. From her work ethic, to her morals, to the way she walks and talks.

"It's a thousand dollars a night."

Her eyes get so big, dilating so the green almost disappears. "What did you say?"

"I'll pay you a thousand dollars a night."

Her hands flex on my shoulders. "For how long?"

"As long as you want." And I mean that. Even if I manage to get my fill of her in a month or two, this is my sister-in-law's best friend and an all-around fantastic woman. I'll pay her to dance for as long as she needs.

"Do I wear clothes while I'm in the cage?"

I chuckle at that. "More than you've got on now," I answer and then stop laughing as I realize, I might have to buy her a full body suit. No other man is touching this skin.

She's melting into me again. Kim's drug is offering to do things for her. Take care of a need, even if she doesn't like taking charity.

Also noted…

I lick at that spot behind her ear and she hums out her pleasure, her arms fully wrapping around my neck.

Yeah, baby. That's it. Come to Leo.

She's skittish. Should have realized that the first night. But I know now. The trick will be just to keep her close, keep her happy. Give her enough to secure her wants and needs without it being so much that's she's suspicious or insulted.

"So if I only dance like five times, I can just quit?"

Hell no. "Yeah, baby, however long you want."

"And…" Her arms loosen from around my neck, her hands come to my shoulders again as she pushes back. "And I don't need to sleep with you to keep the job, do I?"

My teeth clench together. I should have seen that one coming. She's clearly worried about being a good girl. "No. It's not a requirement but it can be a nice side perk."

She frowns, pushing off my lap. "I don't sleep with my bosses."

My brows lift but I don't chase. I stay back in my chair, my legs spread wide as she balances on my lap. "Clearly. You don't sleep with hardly anyone. How long ago was Bobby?"

A flush rises in her cheeks. "We dated freshman year."

She's been three years without sex? What is she, a camel? "And what made you change your mind for me the first time?"

"The only time?"

I don't answer. That is not going to be the only time.

She sighs. "I wanted to know what it felt like for a man to actually give me an…"

That's got me on my feet, her in my arms, pressed down my length. "Was that your first orgasm, princess?"

Now her cheeks are flaming red and the color spreads down her chest, under her tank top. "Delivered by someone else."

The very idea of her touching herself, masturbating, makes me insane. I want to watch so badly that I grind my teeth to keep from adjusting my cock. Yeah, we're doing that very soon.

But it's made her shy again and she pulls away, creating space between us.

"Can you admit," I say low and deep, moving closer as she backs into the counter. "That it was good enough that you want it again?"

Her mouth opens and then closes, her nipples rock hard, her eyes dilate. "I can't..."

I place my hands on the counter on either side of her. "Come in this afternoon and audition." I'd have her come right now, this very minute, before she has time to think, but I've got plans to slink into a corner at Toni Carcetti's casino and watch the comings and goings.

She lets out a long breath, her arms wrapping around her own ribs, covering those nipples. "Fine."

A little triumph surges through me. No, I didn't convince her to go back into her room to let me eat her out until she screamed my name. But I am seeing her again.

Level one, complete.

CHAPTER EIGHT

LEO

THE REST of my afternoon wasn't nearly as fruitful. Despite three hours and four club sodas, Toni never showed at the casino. I'm looking for a regular schedule, or a gap in his security, some way I can plan an attack that is sure not to fail and doesn't involve his family.

But so far, no luck.

Now, I'm holding my clipboard, trying for all the world to pay attention to the dancer in front of me. What was her name again?

Does it even matter?

I scan down the list, seeing Kim on the sheet. My fingers tighten on the pen. My cock twitches from just reading her name. I press two fingers into my eyes. What the hell is wrong with me that even seeing a K on a piece of paper has me in knots?

"Still sexually frustrated, I see," Jake calls from behind me before he comes to take a seat next to me.

I scowl. "I told you. This is not your hunting ground."

Jake grimaces back. "You know, I was all for you giving up drinking until I realized you were going to turn into a grandmother."

"Not a grandmother," Roman says, filing in on the other side. "More like a really bossy mom."

"You mean like the mom you two didn't have?" my cousin Luke adds as he sits next to Roman. Luke is also a Kincaid.

Jake and my dad were brothers, but there is a third. Nick Kincaid. He's retired to Florida. The soft prick.

Luke is his son. He's been around my whole life, and he knows that my mother's only love was the bottle. Vodka, more specifically.

I let out a rumble of frustration. I don't have time for this. "So you're here to insult me for quitting the bottle and to remind me how much my mom loved it?"

Roman frowns. He was only ten when our mom died in a car crash. It hit him hardest, I think. "We're here to give you an update."

I hold up my hand to stop the music and dismiss the dancer in front of me.

She goes with several backwards glances. Once the room is cleared, I sit back in my chair. "What's up?"

It's Jake who begins. "We're having a few issues with our special project."

I scrub a hand down my face. Their special project is my special project too. They just don't know I've been working on it.

It all started with my dad. I inherited my ability to just blow life up from him. Fucking a boss's wife was a stupid idea. I can admit that. But when Toni Carcetti, the head of the Italian mafia had my dad killed, I swore I'd make that guy pay.

I tried last month, and I was kind of successful. I managed to get his top hitman, Giovani Vendetti in jail, but I was also drinking all the time and nearly blew up Mason and Charlotte in the process.

Mason, he's grown our business up to a level that we can afford revenge, but only if we're smart about it. Or...if one of us decides to take the fall. That's me. I'm gonna be the fall guy.

Because in getting Vendetti arrested, I stirred the pot with the whole Italian mafia. And Vendetti, he bombed my brother's apartment building to get back at me. It was fine, Mason built the place to withstand far worse attacks. But between Vendetti's arrest and the bombing, I know what I have to do to protect my family.

They can't be attacking us like that. Especially now that Charlotte has entered our lives. All the other families who do business in our space need to know not to fuck with us.

Roman's been working with the Dukes. New players who came here from England.

Luke's been handling the Russian Bratva.

And Jake…he's been trying to apply the pressure to the Italians. But what he doesn't know, is I've got my own ideas and plans. And they're going to be the difference.

"What issue?" I ask, snapping the pen in half and getting ink all over my fingers.

"Chill, Leo," Roman warns.

But I don't have a chance to answer as Melissa, my dance manager pops her head in. "I've got the next one ready."

"Send her in," I growl out.

I instantly regret the words because Melissa has chosen Kim for the next audition. She's in this tiny black leotard, her hair in this high ponytail, not the soft curls she had this morning. It's straight and very dramatic. Even standing in the room, she's miles above every woman who has ever auditioned.

By the way the guys next to me still, I know they know it too. Or maybe they just recognize her.

"Fuck me," Jake mutters. "I forgot how beautiful she is."

So clearly, it's both.

"What is she doing here?" Roman asks, but Luke, a true dog, leans over Roman to ask me a question.

"Is Kim the screamer?"

My fists are clenched so tight I could make diamonds, as a small snarl rips from my lips. "Careful."

But Jake and Roman have caught on and I can feel the disapproval rolling off all of them. They know I hooked up with Charlotte's best friend.

Kim moves to the center of the room. "Hi," she gives all of them a little wave.

No one waves back.

"What are you dancing to, Kim?" I ask, just to keep this moving along.

She runs a tongue over her lips. "Um. Dua Lipa. 'Houdini.'"

I give a curt nod. Why did my family have to show up today? Now? She takes a stance, hands over her head, back arched, ass out, and I hear Jake hiss under his breath.

The music starts up and she slowly lowers her hands and then she does this move where she rolls her head, sending her ponytail in this aggressive arch before the rest of her body follows. It's sexy and stunning, her skill undeniable.

I'm transfixed. Kim is beautiful just standing. But in motion...I lose every thought as I just watch. I'm not even sure I remember to breathe.

All too soon, the song comes to an end, and she stops, standing before us again.

I think I'm supposed to talk here but words have completely failed me. I know Kim wants to be a ballerina but that was just...

"Well?" she finally asks. "Do you think I'll pass as a cage dancer?"

Roman nudges me, so that I remember to speak. "Yeah. Yeah. You'll pass."

A relieved smile pulls at her lips. "Great. I know I sounded skeptical this morning but..." Her hands twist together. "I really appreciate this, Leo. I wasn't sure how I was going to pay..." She trails off, her hand fluttering. "Thank you."

"Welcome," I answer, clenching and unclenching my ink-stained hand. "You can see Melissa to fill out the forms. Rehearsals start tomorrow at two. There isn't much to it, you mostly do your own moves."

She gives another nod. "Thanks again," then she waves to everyone else, "nice to see all of you."

Before I know it, she's gone.

But I am not alone. Three sets of eyes turn to me, and I know the conversation isn't over. I'd much rather discuss the Italians.

"So wait..." Luke starts. "You're doing her a favor?"

My shoulders relax a little. "She has a class she can't pay for, and she needs money."

"And you know that how?" Jake asks, all fun and games gone. Jake is a hard man when he needs to be. And I know the truth. He's been at the club more because the family is worried I'll fuck up again. They're right.

"Chandra, the blonde from last week, is her roommate."

"Why didn't she just ask Mason to pay for it? I know he considers her his responsibility. Kim is Charlotte's only family."

The idea of Mason taking care of her, further irritates me.

"I don't think she likes taking favors," I rumble back, because I would just pay for the class if she'd let me.

Roman shakes his head. "Do not piss off Mason."

"Mason shouldn't piss me off," I retort, but I get the point. Kim is dangerous territory, and as usual, this is probably going to bite me in the ass. My dad's DNA runs strong in me, if it wasn't obvious.

No one answers that. Instead, Luke gets back on topic. "You want to help Kim, fine. But keep your dick out of it."

What I do with my dick is my business. And Kim's. If I'm lucky.

"Tell me what you came to say..." I turn to Jake.

"The Italians have rebuffed every attempt at communication, even with the amount of money they owe us," he grits out. "It can only mean one thing."

"War is coming." I scrub a hand over my face. I got this ball rolling and I know how I'm going to finish it.

"Soon," Roman agrees. "They're clearly getting ready to make a move."

My window of opportunity is closing. Hopefully I get a little more time before my life goes to hell.

"My guess is that you'll be their primary target, since you're the one who got Vendetti arrested, and you're the one who gave the police the information that led to the arrest."

Yeah. I really knew how to stir up a beehive.

"Mason is calling in their bank notes, which means taking their casino."

It's the right play, but Jake is also correct. I'm likely a target. My eyes drift to the door Kim just exited. I can't afford to be distracted, but I just wanted a bit of softness before I make my move. Because the one I'm planning, means I'll most likely end up in jail.

I wrap up auditions and leave Temptation, making my way down the strip and into Toni's largest casino, the Diamond.

I get there early enough to take a corner booth that is reasonably shadowed, my baseball cap pulled down low.

The waitress grimaces when I order a sparkling water, but I give her a small wink and a twenty. "Keep the change."

She smiles at me, hustling off to get my water when the large double doors on the far side of the casino floor open, several men in gaudy suits appear and I only need to give them the barest glance to know it's the Carcetti family.

I pull my hat lower as I watch the group of them cross the floor. Big Toni is in the lead, his nephew little Anthony at his elbow. Little Anthony has the slicked back hair and greasy smile that makes him look like the piece of shit he is. His usual toothpick hangs out of his mouth. Little Anthony is his uncle's dirty man, doing all the jobs no man with a conscience wants to touch.

He killed a man right out in the open two years ago, shooting a member of the Russian Bratva in our club. He's got no shame and no fear. It makes him dangerous and unpredictable.

They stop for a minute, heads bent together in conversation. Toni and his crew are earlier than I expected, which makes me shift with a bit of irritation. I should have known the Italians wouldn't keep regular schedules. They don't do anything with discipline.

Not that I'm one to talk.

But it means my plan might need some revamping. I can't plan an ambush if I don't know when he's coming and going.

Which only leaves me one option. I know where Toni lives, I've followed him home. But the only way to get to him without hurting his family is to attack the car when he's in transit.

He'll have guards…

Which means I'll be fighting multiple men. I don't want to ask my family to help me. None of them will be accessories for this crime.

With a growl of frustration, I push my hat up, rubbing my forehead.

When I move my hand, I swear I catch Little Anthony's eye. He's looking right at me.

I pull my hat back down, ducking my head, and when I look up, they are passing me by, Little Anthony's gaze straight ahead.

They move on and I get up before my water even arrives. It's time for another plan.

I know the clock is ticking. I will get my revenge on Toni Carcetti. And, for once, I will make my family's life better.

CHAPTER NINE

KIM

I DRAG myself to the first rehearsal, still not able to shake my exhaustion. The idea that I might see Leo perks me up a bit.

Not that I'm sleeping with him again, but a girl can dream…

He's still smoking hot and every time he touches me, I turn into a puddle of want.

At some point, when I was lying awake in bed at like two in the morning, thinking about him, I was going through all kinds of justifications.

Like if we have sex three or four more times, could I tell my mom he was my boyfriend?

But then I remind myself, it's not about creating a veneer, it's about actually living a reality.

I don't sleep around.

Still…at twenty-two, is two guys really out of bounds? And again, if we're hooking up regularly, isn't that better than a one-night stand?

Which is how I brainstorm some new rules. Granted, it's middle of the night logic, but I think it holds. While I work for him, no sex.

Melissa scheduled me for Thursday, Friday, and Saturday nights. If I could work for four weeks, that would be twelve thousand dollars. If I keep my job at Rebel's, I'll have enough money to take my class, and then move to New York. Charlotte isn't going with me like we originally planned, but I can find other dancers to room with once I get there and I'll even have a nest egg to get myself started.

It was a solid plan even if thinking about moving and leaving Vegas just made me more tired.

But I digress.

What did not fill me with exhausted dread was the idea that in between working for Leo and leaving for New York…maybe we could hang out some.

The idea of being with him was the opposite of tiring. With Leo every nerve ending came alive, and now I'm wide awake at three in the morning.

It was easier now that I knew he hadn't slept with Chandra. And that he'd left me his number like he promised. And somehow having an end date where I leave Vegas makes it easier too.

I know that Leo isn't the forever guy, just like I know when he loses interest it's really going to hurt.

Even understanding he isn't the commitment type, I worry about the end of dating Leo. When things got messy with Bobby, it really messed me up.

Like every bad thought I'd had about myself was actually true.

I finally fall asleep but it's restless and I'm ready to get up when my alarm goes off, even though I'm exhausted.

I walk through the doors at Temptation, making my way to the room where all the dancers get ready. Each of us has a locker and a vanity. In mine is a box with my name on it.

A few of the girls are milling about, and I wonder if I should ask them if everyone got this kind of treatment, a gift box that looks high end, when Melissa walks in the door.

"Hey, Kim," she gives me a friendly wave. She's a curvy brunette who is probably ten years older than me, I wave back. She's really pretty and really nice. "I see you found your uniform."

I look down at the box, suddenly curious about what's inside. I slide off the ribbon, taking off the lid.

Black leather fills the inside and I lift out the piece. It's a full leather bodysuit that goes from wrist to ankle with a crew neck. I stare at it. This thing probably cost more than I make in a month.

"Don't worry," Melissa waves with another smile. "Each of the cages has an air vent above it that blows cool air directly on you so you don't overheat. You get to set the temperature."

I blink in surprise as the other dancers crowd close checking out my clothing. "Oh wow, that's a really nice one," another redhead gushes. "My ass completely hangs out of mine."

That sounds more like Leo's style and I wonder why there is so much...fabric...on my costume. Not that I'm complaining.

"Kim is a family friend of the Kincaids," Melissa says by way of explanation, and I grimace. Will the other dancers dislike me because they think I'll get preferential treatment?

"Leo is doing me a favor. I'm trying to get to New York."

I hear some gasps, but Melissa waves her hand. "Kim got an interview at the New York Ballet."

The other girls begin babbling at once, everyone sounded really excited, but Melissa keeps going. "And I saw your audition. You are definitely doing us a favor. You're amazing."

"Thanks." If only the ballet had thought so. But the words don't sting like they did even a few days ago.

Melissa clears her throat. "Today, I'll give you the playlist. You'll get to know the song set and come up with your own moves. It's just good to have some prepared. Tomorrow, you'll do a rehearsal in costume. And Thursday you'll start."

"Great," I say with a smile.

The redhead leans forward. "I'm Samantha and I'll show you how we enter and exit the cages. It's kind of crazy until you get used to it."

I look down at the leather suit. This whole thing is all kinds of crazy, including the money.

I'm wearing my leotard under my leggings and short sweater. I take off my ballet flats and pull some heels from my bag. There is no way I'm dancing in the cage in flats.

My black leotard has cap sleeves, but it's got a ballerina neck that cuts pretty low and it cuts kind of high on my hip.

I slip on the heels and adjust the ponytail and follow Samantha to a back set of stairs.

We climb up what must be three stories until we enter a large room that's open on one end, overlooking the dance floor below. "No way."

"Cool, right?" Samantha says with a smile. "There's a plexiglass railing but it has several breaks in it, each break for one of the cages. We load in the cages up here and then they raise and lower us as we dance."

We walk toward the edge, and I get a little vertigo looking down as I reach for the rail. Each cage is on a hydraulic pole but currently they are all on the ground, so nothing is between us and the edge where there is no railing.

That's when I feel a hand on my hip. I don't even have to look to know it's Leo. I can feel him, smell him, long before I see him.

With his hand on my hip, he curls me toward his body, settling me into his side. My face heats as Samantha's eyes go wide. "Mr. Kincaid."

He gives her a nod, before he turns to me. "There will be a cage operator who helps you in and out while he runs the cage. Is that all right? You look a little out of sorts."

I nod. "I'm sure it will be fine."

"Afraid of heights?"

I shake my head. "No. I don't know what happened. I've just been off. I got a little dizzy."

A small line appears between his brows. "You said that yesterday. Have you told Charlotte? Seen a doctor?"

"So you and Mr. Kincaid like *know* know each other," Samantha says softly.

It must look so bad that he's holding me like this. Questioning my health. I try to step back but he keeps me tight.

"I'll take it from here," Leo says, still staring at me, not even looking at Samantha. Then he reaches over and pushes a button, the sound of a motor firing up as the cage clanks into motion.

"Thank you, Samantha," I call after her. She gives me a small wave before she reaches the stairs and disappears.

I thump Leo on the chest. "You can't do that."

"Do what?"

"Look," I let out an exasperated sigh, "I've worked with a lot of groups of women, and they don't like it when they think the boss is playing favorites."

He has the decency to frown. "So I should give Samantha extra dances and extra pay tonight?"

"Yes, please," I softly answer before I see his nostrils flare.

"You know I love it when you say please."

"Leo," I gasp. Then I clear my throat. "Maybe I should call you Mr. Kincaid?"

"Only if you want me to put you over my knee."

I stare at him, not entirely hating the idea if I'm being honest. But the cage reaches the top and I turn my head to stare. It's larger than I thought, plenty of room for me to move and I feel much safer at the top with the cage blocking the opening in the rail. There is a four-inch gap between the cage and the landing, but Leo's got my hand firmly in his as I move away, stepping over the gap and into the cage.

There isn't even any music, but I grab a bar in the middle and swing myself around, my back arching as I pivot on my toes.

"Jesus Christ, I'm going to hell." Leo is still in the opening, his eyes glued to my body. "You are way too good at that."

I give him a sassy little grin. "This was your idea."

His gaze turns so hot, it could melt my leotard off. Sex with Leo was amazing, but I have this vision of both of us actually being naked, of our skin sliding together, and the next swing of my hips goes out even further.

He lets out this growling sound. "Cue the music."

A popular dance song fires up and I listen for a second before I start to move. I can't help it, I keep looking at him and he's devouring me with his gaze. My body pulses with that same raw desire I had that night at the wedding.

This man is like a drug…

My neck arches, the movement carrying all down my body.

A muscle ticks in his jaw and my gaze slides down to see the erection in his tight jeans. I nearly lose my footing then.

“Cage coming down,” he yells and then pushes another button.

I hold on as it starts to move, the speed slow and the motion steady enough that I quickly adjust.

That’s when I notice, Leo wasn’t the only person watching.

Bartenders, waitstaff, dancers have all stopped to watch me as the song changes and I switch the rhythm and the moves.

The cage starts going back up, my body tightening at the idea of seeing Leo again. The energy between us is electric and I briefly wonder how I’m even going to hold out a month.

It’s one thing when I didn’t have to see him. But now…

I hit the top and he stops the cage, reaching his hand in to help me out. “Is that it?”

“For cage practice…yes.” He doesn’t pull me close this time and once I’m out of the cage, he doesn’t wrap an arm around me. “The rest of rehearsal will be on the floor.”

I nod, trying to fortify myself for his next offensive attack. But it doesn’t come.

He drops my hand and walks away, only giving me a quick, “Good luck,” over his shoulder.

I’d been readying myself to tell him that we weren’t happening yet. That we needed to wait. Ever since I met Leo, he’s been chasing me like the lion he is.

So I’m completely unprepared for him to be the one who walks away.

And I have to admit, it makes me want to chase him. I start across the room to follow him down the stairs to the dance floor, but I can’t keep up. I am in three-inch heels. When I get to the bottom, he’s gone.

I don’t ask, instead, I join the rest of rehearsal. The girls are all good dancers, but I can tell by the way they watch me, that everyone thinks I'm special.

"How do you do that with your hips?" Samantha asks as she comes to stand next to me.

Something softens and warms in me. I love dancing but there is something about teaching moves that really makes me excited. "I can show you."

"Really?" Samantha exclaims and several other girls come in. I look back, giving them all a smile. "It's a pop that starts in the toes..."

For the next fifteen minutes, I show the other cage dancers how to up their game with their hips.

It's so weird, I've been avoiding this kind of stuff for as long as I can remember. What does it say about me that this is where I excel?

I try to shake off the thoughts. I'm not here for Leo. I'm here to make money, finish my degree, and get out of Vegas.

And I've got a performance to prepare.

CHAPTER TEN

Leo

I've been skulking around my own damned club all week.

Normally, I spend at least half a day at each of our ten clubs, tallying books, checking ledgers, hiring staff etc.

But I'm nearly as obsessed with Kim as I am on revenge which is really saying something. I've got to have sex with this woman again. Soon.

I'm haunting Temptation and peeking from behind curtains to catch a glimpse of Kim dancing, like some lovesick teenager.

Or some creepy perve instead of the super-rich owner of some of Las Vegas premium real estate.

Tonight, my little dancer performs at the club for the first time.

Yesterday she did a rehearsal in the full suit I picked out for her myself. I wanted her skin covered.

But the way that leather fits her like a second skin, she looks even more like sex on a stick then she did in a leotard. I might be regretting my choice.

With the evening approaching, I can feel the anticipation building inside my stomach. She's going to rock this, and I'm going to have to try and not kill the men who make a pass at her. And there are going to be so many...

I know I'm not usually this possessive, and I get it's a problem. I don't know what makes her so different, but I can't turn it off.

Is it the fact that she's always running away from me, or the fact that she's amazingly gorgeous, talented, and still somehow sweet underneath her tough exterior? Is it the mind-blowing sex? Or is it that she seems to need me so damned much even if she doesn't want to admit it?

Whatever it is, I can't get enough of her, even when I'm not touching her. I blow a breath through my nose. This is one night I could use a drink.

I've been two months without having one, and honestly, after getting over the initial loss, I've liked not being altered.

My temper has always been a problem, and without alcohol, I'm way more in control.

But as my knee bounces, I wish I had something to take the edge off.

If not a drink, maybe a good solid session between the sheets.

I know Kim is in the back getting ready right now. She's so close I could just go collect her up and then take her to my office. I'd love to sink deep inside her.

But she had a point. Neither my family, nor the staff here, would take kindly to us obviously hooking up and so I've been keeping my distance.

But my patience is getting so thin.

I hear the doors open, and the club instantly fills with people. We're the sort of place that has a line, even at ten when all the other clubs are dead. I resist the urge to go back and check on her. I wait until I can hear the floor is packed and then the techno music sounds.

That's the cue that the dancers are about to start.

Only then, do I head out of my office and onto the floor.

I've got a spot at the corner of the bar that I can slip in and out, see everything and hardly be seen.

I take my place, Mike, the bartender, giving me a sparkling water as the strobes start up, the cages rising.

The crowd is already going nuts as the cages hit the top, the lights fading away.

And then they surge back on, illuminating the cages, the dancers in place.

I see Kim, striking a pose in the center cage, her long lean body making my balls ache.

But I'm not the only one who notices the new dancer.

The crowd lets out a roar as the first song begins and Kim starts to dance. I'm sure the other dancers move too, but who can watch them? My eyes are glued to her, and I lean forward, drinking in every second she's performing.

"Wow," Mike says from next to me. He's watching too and not serving drinks. "That new dancer is really something."

"Back to work," I bark out and push up from stool. I shouldn't do it, I never go upstairs at night, but I find myself stomping up the stairs to the upper landing.

The next set of dancers is already waiting. They won't go in the cages for another fifteen minutes, the girls getting changed out every half hour or so. But they know the drill. Everyone waits at the ready. The night moves seamlessly. This is why Temptation is a success.

I walk around the edge of the room until I'm at the corner of the rail where I can see all the cages floating up and down.

The crowd is going wild and several of the spotlights are trained on Kim. My arms cross, my hands are clenched into tight balls under my elbows.

Finally, the cages start up and I stomp toward hers.

Her operator stops her cage at the top and reaches his hand in to help her step out.

But he's not looking at her, not watching her steps. The crowd is pulsing and cheering for her and he's staring out at them grinning.

I pick up speed as Kim steps out of the cage, her first foot landing fine but her second doesn't. The ball of her foot is on the platform but the heel.

I see her wobble, her heel floating over thin air. She tightens her hand in the operator's but I'm there before he can even respond.

The fear in her eyes is enough to make my blood run cold as I yank her from his grasp and into my arms.

I feel her stuttering gasp, her eyes so wide and her lips parted in surprise, but I barely look at her before I'm snarling at the operator. "What the fuck?"

He's gone completely pale, not that I care, and I'm about to tear him open when Kim's hands slide down my biceps. "I should have been watching where I stepped."

That brings my gaze to hers. "It's his job to see to your safety."

"I know, but it's my job too. Yell at me for not watching where I put my feet."

Yell at her? Is she crazy? All I want to do is hug her to my chest and then kiss her senseless. And just like that, my anger evaporates as I pick her up and carry her toward the stairs.

"Leo," she gasps, hands tightening on my arms. "You can't just carry me. Everyone's watching..."

"Let them." All right, maybe I'm still not thinking completely clearly. But the idea of her falling has my blood pumping.

I stomp down the stairs and straight into my office, slamming the door behind me. It's barely closed before I press her back to the thick wood, our chests grinding together.

And then I kiss her.

Because I'd go insane if something had happened to her.

She kisses me back, her mouth as hungry as mine as our tongues tangle together. One of her legs wraps around my waist.

I'd like to feel this woman in a bed, I really would, but she feels so good against a wall or a door, her legs around me.

My fingers slide up the leather encasing her leg to grab her ass and hold it in my hands. But she doesn't feel as good in the suit as she normally does, and I'm suddenly pissed I bought this thing. It should have been a bikini.

"Leo," she says into my mouth. "Leo...we can't."

I pull back to stare at her. "Why not?"

"Because…"

I know that it's a bad idea. I've been through all the reasons myself. But in this moment, I've forgotten them. What I remember… I'm a man, she's a woman, neither of us is married. And the attraction between us is electric. What reason could she possibly have that trumps that?

"You're my boss."

I let out a curse. It's a good reason. "Every boss on the Las Vegas strip is fucking a dancer."

But I see the hurt in her eyes the moment the words leave my mouth and I know I shouldn't have said them.

She's pushing me away, her feet slide to the floor, her hands smooth the leather, before she opens the door and steps out without another word.

How can she not know that I never act like this? That what is happening between us is…different? I don't want to say special because the word makes me uncomfortable.

"Kim." I reach for her hand before she's completely out the door. "Don't go. Not yet."

She shakes her head and that's when I catch the wetness shining in them. Fuck me, did I make her cry? I pull her back into the room and close the door again, but this time I just hold her, one hand at her neck, the other around her back.

"I'm sorry. I think it was the near fall…I'm weirdly emotional."

"Don't apologize," I hum against her ear. "I'm the dick who said the words. And I didn't mean them like that, I only meant no one would think it's weird."

"I know how you meant it. It's my thing that I worry guys won't respect me."

I lean back to look in her eyes then. I don't know what's going on between us, but I know this woman needs to understand she is so far beyond any other that I've met. "If some D-bag doesn't see your worth, that's because he is an idiot, not because you're not special. Because you are, gorgeous."

The shy smile I get makes my chest swell. "Thank you."

I lean in to kiss her again, but she turns her face to the side, showing me her cheek. I kiss it, leaning my forehead on her temple. "I'm dying here, Kim."

I feel her smile. "Once I have tuition money and a little extra, I'll quit. Then I'll be in Vegas all fall while I retake that class."

Is she offering me a window? I've never allowed a woman to set parameters like that, but my pulse thrums with victory at the idea that she's willing to let me back in her bed at all. Not that we've actually been in a bed but my point stands.

"What happens after the fall?" Why do I even care? I've never been with one woman longer than a month. The attraction will burn itself out and I'll return to my Vendetti vendetta.

She shrugs. "My mom always wanted to be a professional ballet dancer and now I'm almost there. Maybe."

It's an odd thing to say…her mom wanted to be a ballet dancer. What does Kim want?

I slide my fingers down her spine. "Counter offer."

She looks at me, her brows rising. "What?"

"I won't pick you up in front of the other dancers and I'll mostly leave you alone at the club. In exchange…"

But her eyes are narrowing. "Leo."

I hear the tapping of heels outside my office and they stop in front of my door. No one knocks, but my gaze cuts to the clock. It's nearly time for Kim to go back on. With a sigh, I let her go, but as she opens the door, I deliver my parting comment.

"This conversation isn't over."

CHAPTER ELEVEN

KIM

THE REST of the night passes in a blur of loud music and hard dancing and my body is complete jelly by the time the night is over.

It's two in the morning and I just want to crawl into bed.

I make my way to the locker room and attempt to peel myself out of the suit. Samantha ends up helping me.

I was a little worried we wouldn't be cool after Leo interrupted her tour of the upper deck.

But she gives me a friendly smile as she tugs the leather encasing my arm. "So…" she says finally dislodging the upper half so I can shimmy the rest of the suit down my hips and off my legs. "You and Mr. Kincaid?"

"No," I rush to say. Then I grimace. He pulled me into his office where we stayed for a while. "I mean…maybe. I'm not sure."

Samantha gives me a wink. "I've been working here for a few months, and I've never seen him show interest in a dancer."

My shoulders unwind, softening. I really appreciate knowing that I'm not just some flavor of the week. "Thanks."

"Hey girls," Melissa calls from just to my right, her eyes lingering on me. "Pay time."

Each girl gets a check and then cash on top. Bonuses, I guess.

Samantha gets hers and I see her eyes bug out and then meet mine. There is a note that her eyes scan over. "He gave me a bonus for helping you. How cool is that?"

"That's awesome," I answer. "Is that where all the cash is from?"

She shakes her head. "There are buttons on the floor that match our cages. If people like you, they press them and give you tips."

My brows shoot up as each of the girls collect their money. I'm at the end of the line and when I finally reach Melissa, she winks. "You need to see Mr. Kincaid for your pay."

Crap.

Twisting my hands together, I start for his office. We've got to talk about how he keeps giving me special attention.

I knock on his partially open door. "Leo?"

He opens the door and sweeps his hand inside for me to enter.

I close it behind me, crossing my arms like I'm fortifying myself. "Why did I have to collect my pay here?"

His brow lifts as he raises a large stack of cash. "First, I'm keeping you off the books so that you're not paying taxes, and second," he gives the stack a little wave, "you made three times the tips of every other girl. I didn't think you'd want them to see that."

My mouth drops open as I reach for the money. "How much?" I whisper, touching the fold of bills.

"I promised you a thousand, you made another eight hundred in tips."

I blink, trying to process that one more night like this and I could almost pay for my class. Why didn't I sell my dignity sooner?

I go to pull the money out of his hand but he doesn't let it go. "Third."

"There's a third?" I say tugging a little harder until Leo surrenders the money.

"I'm driving you home."

"What?" I run my hand over the money, feeling silly tears well in my eyes again. It would take two months for me to earn this at Rebel's.

"I know you won't pay for an Uber and I'm not letting you walk with that kind of cash." It's not a request, not a question. And honestly, I don't argue. I could say I'm too tired but holding almost half of my tuition has eliminated the exhaustion that was pulling at my limbs.

"All right."

"No fight?" He steps closer, running his fingertips down my spine.

"Not tonight," I answer as I shake my head, clutching the cash in both hands against my chest. "Tonight I just want to enjoy one of my problems disappearing."

He grins at me, dropping his forehead to mine. "Come on, let's get you home."

I didn't bring my bag into his office or any of my other stuff, so I hand him back the money. "I need to get my bag." I don't want to walk past the other dancers with this.

He stuffs the cash in his front pocket, and I stop midway out the door. Two grand is still smaller than his erection in his pants.

He sees me staring, his grin turning wicked. "Come on, princess. Let's go."

I jerk my chin in agreement and rush to the locker room. It's already cleared out except for Melissa who straightens when she sees me. "Really great job tonight."

"Thank you," I answer, genuinely surprised. "And thanks for hiring me. It's really great working here."

She laughs. "I didn't hire you, to be fair. That was all Mr. Kincaid. But he clearly knew what he was doing. Always does. Since he took over the club, he's doubled our profits." She gives me a wink. "And you are obviously very special to him."

I stare at her, wondering if I should believe the words. But they also give me a little tingle of concern. Am I worried about the favoritism he's showing me? Or something else in Melissa's words?

She closes a few of the locker doors and tosses some towels in a basket in the corner. I grab my bag, say goodnight, and head back to

Leo's office. He meets me in the hall, and we head out the back door where a sleek black sports car waits.

My brows raise as he clicks a button on the key fob and then opens the door for me so that I slide in.

The seats are surprisingly comfortable, not that I relax into them. For the first time in actual weeks, I feel awake.

I guess money can do that. But I'm restless and as Leo climbs in, he hands me my money before he fires up the car.

He pulls out of the club, weaving his way through the Las Vegas streets, neither of us saying much.

My body is humming from the feel of the engine, the money in my bag, and, most of all, the man next to me.

An ache is pulsing between my legs as I watch him drive. It's a standard transmission and he's working the gears back and forth, his movements as fluid and agile as the car itself.

"I have a question," the words pop out of my mouth before I can take them back. But the ache is building, energy humming through me, and I watch his hand on the stick shift, my lips so dry I have to lick them.

A wild thought is working through my brain. I'm feeling giddy again, like I did at the wedding.

And today has been so great, I don't want it to end. And honestly, I don't want to spend another night in my bed alone…thinking about him and what he might be doing in his.

"What's that?"

I run my hands over my thighs, knowing that I am about to push us even deeper into the grey space we've been in since he showed up at my apartment. And I know this is where trouble happens. "Do you think…"

"Princess," he growls, a low rumble that makes me even hotter.

"Would…umm…masturbating…together…count as sex?"

His gaze slides to mine, his eyes holding the sort of promise that makes my breath hitch. And then, he snaps the blinker and turns left, heading back toward 55. My brow crinkles in confusion. "Where are we going?"

"My place."

"But…" I turn sideways in the seat, to study his profile.

"Masturbation doesn't count," he answers. "Definitely not." And then he punches the accelerator.

"But you know that means that we're not going to have—" I'm trying to be clear because that's the thing about a man like Leo. You start a ball rolling and there's no stopping it.

"Watching you touch yourself, princess, will be hot enough for tonight."

For tonight…

Yeah, Leo isn't planning on this being a one-night or two-night thing and that makes me feel better.

Loads of people date for a month or two before they realize they're not right for each other.

I can at least pretend that's what we're doing if I can just ignore my nagging conscience.

Leo steers the car through the thicker traffic that comes with being closer to the strip before he pulls into a high-rise building.

But it's kind of weird because there are almost no cars in the parking garage.

"Mason built it," he answers before I even ask. "We've yet to sell off the units."

"So you live in this building by yourself?"

"Roman, Jake, and Luke all have apartments in here too. And we set up a gym in a fourth. But other than that…"

I look at the garage. It could hold hundreds of cars. What would it be like to have so much money, you don't bother selling a multi-million-dollar project?

I see the flash of a red light and note a security camera in one corner, then another and another. But I don't have time to really look at the pattern because Leo is out of the car and coming around to my side, snapping open the door and reaching for my hand.

His hand is at my back as we approach an elevator.

I blink in surprise as he pushes a button, not on a keypad on the wall, but on his phone, the doors of the elevator slide open.

"Private elevator," he answers as if this explains it.

It's just like the wedding. Just spending time with Leo, I could almost forget about the ridiculous amounts of money this man possesses. I get a little hectic inside… but I don't have a chance to ask many questions because the moment the doors slide closed, Leo pulls me close and then backs me against the wall, his lips finding mine.

I try to tell him that we're not supposed to be making out like this. Ok. Fine. I don't really try.

His mouth feels so good, his tongue sliding against mine, the hard press of him making that ache that's been building all night throb wildly.

I wrap my arms around his neck and twine my fingers into his hair and instead of pushing him away, I pull him closer.

CHAPTER TWELVE

Kim

Just like the last time, it's a completely wild ride as Leo grabs my ass with both hands and grinds our hips together.

I let out a half cry, half moan as I pulse with need. I might orgasm in the elevator if we don't slow down.

His lips are sliding down my neck and I give my head a little shake. "Leo."

"What, gorgeous?"

"We're not supposed to be touching like this."

"But I like touching you."

"It's supposed to be masturbation, remember?"

"Oh, I do. I'm really looking forward to that part."

"I don't want to be the girl who sleeps with her boss."

"There is definitely going to be sleeping after the orgasm. Neither of us is going to want to dress and drive to your apartment," he answers, being intentionally difficult. "And I can't promise I won't kiss a bunch of your skin. Just saying."

I push at him. "I was dancing all night, I'm all sweaty."

I've got a leg hooked around his hips, when did that happen? And he's rubbing me up and down with his stiff cock, as his eyes hold mine. "Hmmm. You're right. A shower is an excellent idea."

I start to protest. That isn't what I meant.

But he lifts me in his arms, the hand he's planted on my ass managing to wrap around my thigh just enough so that he can push his fingertips into my sex with exactly the right amount of force so that I'm arching into him to try to feel more.

I'm barely paying attention as we walk through the dark apartment and into a bathroom.

But when he hits the switch in the bathroom and the lights come on, I gasp. The bathroom is massive, with high-end finishes and a shower big enough for six people.

He sets me down and reaches in to turn on several shower heads before he strips his T-shirt off up over his head.

And then I forget about how impressive the shower is as I take in his massively muscled shoulders and ripped stomach.

He's got a sprinkling of hair on his chest, the kind I want to run my fingers through, and I reach up, but he catches my hand. "Masturbation, remember? Clothes off."

"I see you remember when it suits you." But I pull my tank over my head and then undo my ponytail.

I watch as he kicks off his shoes, and then unbuttons his jeans, shoving them down his hips.

I do the same with my leggings and ballet flats, feeling my cheeks heat a bit. Leo has never seen me naked and the lighting in here hides nothing.

But if I'm worried he won't like what he sees, he lets out a rumble of appreciation, his gaze sliding down me. "You're so beautiful."

"Right back at you." Leo isn't a man...he's a god. The muscles don't end with his chest and abs, they keep going down his body, to his lean hips and powerful thighs. No wonder he carries me around like I weigh nothing.

My eyes settle on his thick erection, the one I said wouldn't be inside me tonight, and I whimper with regret.

But he doesn't give me a chance to change my mind as he opens the shower door again, and ushers me inside.

I'm under the hot spray, his body pressed to mine as he kisses my cheek and then grabs some shampoo, squirting some into his hand and bringing it to my head.

I laugh at the quarter sized amount. "It's going to take a lot more than that."

He grins as he runs a hand down my head over the hair now wet and sticking to my back. The shampoo he's squeezed out, doesn't even begin to suds up for the amount of hair I have.

I take the bottle and pour a generous amount into my palm, beginning to soap up the long strands. It's going to be a curly mess in the morning, but I'll worry about that later because as I start to scrub through my hair, I realize my arms are up over my head and my body is on full display.

Leo slides his gaze down my torso and then he grabs the soap and starts washing me, his hands everywhere.

He skims them over my back and down my legs, bending low and reminding me of that first night when he was also bent down in front of me.

My sex gives another needy throb as his hand sweeps up the inside of my thigh. It's on the tip of my tongue to take back my own request to masturbate. It's a loophole anyway, a desperate attempt from a horny woman.

But instead of pushing his hands between my legs, he runs them back over my hips and up my belly, scrubbing over my ribs until he's cupping both my breasts, tweaking the nipples.

"Leo," I gasp because it feels so good.

"I'm just washing," he replies, like I was going to accuse him of not keeping to the spirit of our agreement. I think I'm past caring as I rinse the shampoo from my hair, Leo spending an inordinate amount of time washing my chest.

"Time to rinse," he rumbles close to my ear as he spins me around so he can pull my back to his front.

Then he grabs the shower head from its cradle, and I realize it's mobile with a long cord, as he starts spraying down my body, rinsing all the soap off, until he points the spray between my legs.

And then my eyes roll back in my head because...wow. "I need to get one of these," I hitch as my knees go weak.

But Leo is ready, and his other arm wraps about my torso, holding me up. My hands press against the shower wall, my cheek and upper chest following, resting against the cool tile, to help support my weight. One of my legs hooks around his calf as my feet come off the floor.

I can feel his erection pushing between my butt cheeks, the spray pummeling my clit, Leo holding me up off the floor, as my body tightens like a violin string.

I can't even imagine what this would feel like if he was inside me while he used the shower head...

I explode, an orgasm ripping through me as I gasp out a sob, crying Leo's name.

"That's it, baby, be loud," he hums in my ear. "Scream out my name."

"Leo," I beg because the water is still hitting me and I can already feel another orgasm building. "Oh God."

"Yeah. Yeah, I am." But then he hangs up the shower head and reaches for the valve, turning it off. I cry out a protest as he laughs in my ear.

He's still supporting my weight with one arm as he opens the door and finally sets me down, wrapping me in a towel that is somehow warm...

And then with another he's drying all my exposed skin. I wish I'd known I was going to get this full spa treatment, I would have done this a lot sooner.

Some deep feminine part of me is in awe that this large, powerful man is washing and drying me like I'm some precious person to him.

"Do you always take such good care—" He lifts me into his arms, cradling my body against his as he carries me out to the bedroom.

"You know you're special, Kim," he whispers into my temple before he pulls back the covers and lays me down on the mattress.

I blink at the words, feeling the sting of another round of tears. I don't know what's up with my leaky eyes today or how Leo knew those were the exact words I needed to hear, but as he opens up my towel, exposing my skin to his gaze, I don't feel self-conscious at all. The only thing I feel is ready.

He's still standing next to the bed, and he grabs his own erection, running his hand up and down the long, thick length.

My lips part because it's amazing and erotic, and I want to touch him like that too.

"You're supposed to be doing this too," he says, his gaze locking with mine. I slide my fingers down my body, his gaze pinging between my hand and my eyes until I brush my own fingertips through my curls and down to the lips. I let out a little moan at the friction.

"Fuck," he rumbles out as I press deeper into my own flesh, my body arching into the touch.

He climbs onto the bed, parting my legs wider as he settles on his knees between my thighs. Pushing them further open, he places a hand over my belly as I keep touching myself, his other hand still working over his erection.

I'm wide open and on full display. I don't care, as the pressure from my fingers tightens my body, moving me toward another orgasm.

"That's it, baby," he whispers, his tempo increasing with mine. "You gonna cum like a good little girl?"

"Yeah," I moan out, my knees softly bending and unbending, the inside of my legs rubbing against his. "God. Yes."

"Not God. Leo. Say it, baby. Say my name."

"Leo," I mewl out. It feels so good, but I want him inside me too. That's what would make this even better.

As if he knows, he slides his hand over my hip and then uses his middle finger to push deep inside me.

My body arches and shudders, the contact amazing as I grip down tightly on his finger.

"Jesus, Kim, how did I even fit inside you?"

I don't answer, I'm too close, too ready to explode, and so instead, I just cry out, "Leo."

"I'm here, baby. I'm right here." His hand is flying over his erection now, the tip appearing and disappearing in his large palm. It's so hot, watching him is what finally tips me over the edge, and I scream out, another orgasm breaking over me.

He starts to cum too, semen slashing over my belly and through my pubic hair.

It's messy and amazing and before I even think about it, I reach down, spreading his cum into my skin.

He watches me, his gaze dark and unreadable, his finger still pumping inside me, his hand still grasping himself.

"Kim."

"Yeah?"

"I meant what I said. I want you to stay tonight."

I hadn't thought about what happened after this at all, so I just nod, glad not to have to worry. He was right. Who would want to get dressed and drive after this? That's probably why he wants me to stay. He said as much…

"All right." He's still inside me, still perched over me, but I slide both my hands up my body and over my head, stretching into the mattress. "Your bed is really comfortable."

He lets go of his cock, to place his hand flat on my belly as he swipes his palm through the drying semen. "You're beautiful."

That pulls my lips into a smile even as I close my eyes. That one burst of energy has gone, the tiredness back and tugging at my limbs. "What time is it? I'm so tired."

"Four," he answers, finally pulling his finger out of me and getting off the bed. I open my eyes to see where he's gone but he's making his way into the bathroom, and he returns a moment later, with a washcloth in hand.

I don't argue when he wipes down my sex, though I do note that he doesn't clean my belly as I roll onto my side and snuggle deeper into the bed.

He joins me a moment later, snuggling his front against my back as he wraps me in his arms. "Get some sleep," he whispers, but I hardly hear him.

I can't remember the last time I was this comfortable.

I know the morning is bound to be awkward but that is a problem for after I get some sleep.

CHAPTER THIRTEEN

LEO

I WAKE AT NINE, a creature of habit, and smile as a curtain of curly red hair blocks my vision. Gotta be honest, I love her red hair. It's bold and beautiful, just like the way she dances. I see flashes of that in her personality too, when she's not busy being insecure.

Kim is in my bed, her body still curled into mine. She's soft and warm, with her tits and belly pressed into my side, her cheek on my chest, and my second thought of the day is how I could actually get used to this. The feel of her in my arms.

Which is crazy. I don't do that. Have snuggly sleepovers.

Except I did do that…and I liked it. No, I more than liked it. I stretch against her, my hand sliding over her hip. I fucking loved it.

She's completely naked and I brush away her hair, lovely as it is, the silky strands catching on my scruff, as I drink in the view. The curves of her body are stunning and she's so beautiful, my chest grows tight.

"Are you awake?" her voice is a sleepy slur, and I kiss the top of her head.

"Yeah. I'm awake. But you don't have to be. I'm going to go work out."

She jerks awake and I kinda hate the way she stiffens. I liked her soft. "Do I need to leave?"

"No," I push her back down into the bed, and turn her so that I'm spooning her body, my front pressed to her back. I kiss her shoulder and then her neck. "The gym is in the building. I'm going to exercise while you get some more sleep. When I'm done, I'm going to make us some smoothies and then we are going to take a shower. After that, I'll drive you home."

"You've got it all planned out," she sighs into the pillow, but she's back to being soft. I like it. I slide my hand over her hip, just tracing her curves. My cock is already hard as a rock and I know I could go with a different plan, one that involves a workout in bed.

"I do." I am sounding like my brother in a way that I actually like. I'll have to figure out who runs the clubs when I'm gone so I can start training them. The idea is to leave my family in a better position than before.

And while I'm playing Mason, I'm going to have to decide how to be at Temptation more the next few weeks while Kim is dancing. Because I don't want her on stage when I'm not there.

Which means being at the other clubs less. She lets out a soft sigh in my arms as I graze her head with another kiss. I'll get reports from the other club managers sent to Temptation and then I'll rework my schedule to visit the less successful clubs on Kim's days off. She's on Temptation's schedule on the busiest days anyway so it's justifiable I'd want to be at the highest-earning club on the weekends.

She goes back to sleep, and I hold her for a few more minutes before I slip from the bed, almost hating to leave her. But a workout helps me stay focused, driven, and level-headed so I make my way down to the gym.

Luke and Roman are there already, both pumping iron.

I sit on the rower, wanting to work up a good sweat before I start lifting, and rowing is my favorite way to do cardio. It works every muscle in my body.

Jake walks in and my brows go up. I've never seen him at the gym before. I do notice that he's got a stogie in his pocket, that he takes out and gives a sniff.

"He's quitting," Roman murmurs low as he walks by. "Cut him a wide path."

Jake not smoking? I shake my head. "I bet its worse than giving up booze."

"I wouldn't know," Jake answers, having overheard me. "You'll have to pry the bourbon from my cold, dead hands."

I smile and keep rowing, pretty content to mind my own business. But the guys have other plans.

They're all working out, but I notice they keep glancing my way...

I can feel my temper flaring. I hate this tiptoe shit. It pisses me off. If they want to ask something, ask it.

"What?" I finally say as I stop the rower, standing. "What is it you want to say?"

"Chill, Leo, we're just curious..." It's Roman who sets down his barbell that he's been lifting. "What's going on with you and Kim?"

My mouth twitches with irritation as my chest puffs, ready for a fight. "What makes you think something is going on?"

"Oh please." Luke drops his dumbbells, a loud thunk echoing through the room. "You've been in a shit mood for a month and now you're all happy this morning? Smiling to yourself while you work out. You got laid. And considering you hired Kim like three days ago, it's pretty easy math."

"I did not get laid." And that is the truth. But Luke's words take some of the sting out of my temper. No one is accusing me of rattling Mason's cage or ruining the business with my crazy schemes.

"So I wouldn't find a naked woman in your bed?" Jake asks with a grin, lifting the smallest dumbbell on the rack. How does he look so fit drinking, smoking, and lifting baby weights?

But I'm back to being pissed. "Try to go in my apartment and find out what happens." I pick up a much larger weight, lifting it with enough menace to let him know he's been warned.

I've made some pretty big mistakes since my father's death. I know that. I probably should have gone off and made them away from the family, processed my anger on my own. Then again, if I'd done that, I might be dead.

But just because I know I've fucked up, doesn't mean these guys can tell me what to do.

"The gym might have been a bad choice for this conversation," Roman says with a sigh before he lifts his hands. "But the truth is..."

"The truth is that Kim is an adult," I say. "And so am I."

"Who you are employing and who is the most important person in the world to Mason's wife other than Mason."

Both true. Not that I didn't know this conversation was about Mason. I shake my head. I've got to stop losing my temper and do what Mason would actually do. He'd reason. He'd win them over with logic rather than try to beat them into submission. I'm working on it. "Fine. I concede both points. But..." I curl the weight, sinking deeper into this idea of winning the guys over. "I am letting her completely run the show."

"You?" Roman asks.

"You?" Luke says at the same time.

"How?" Jake follows.

"She says we can't actually sleep together while she works at the club. It's her rule, not mine."

The guys are all staring at me, so I continue. "And I wouldn't have hired her at all, but she wants to go to New York in January, and she won't take money from me or Mason. I had to hire her to help finance her move."

Jake's eyes narrow as he cocks his head to the right, assessing me. "Are you pussy whipped?"

Fuck that and fuck him. "I will throw this at you."

He takes a step back.

Luke starts adding weights to the squat machine. "So you two are messing around but you're letting her dictate all the terms so that you can finance her future move?"

"That's right," I let out a long breath. "The woman is hellishly hard to nail down. Every time I think I understand the rules, she changes them."

The guys all laugh.

"What's funny?"

"You're dating you," Luke says on a snort.

Maybe I am.

But Roman is the first to recover. "In the name of turning over a new leaf, you ought to tell Mason."

That would sour any good mood.

Mason is going to be a giant pain in the ass about all of this. Still, they're right. If I'm going to convince everyone I'm doing the right thing, I have to be upfront and honest. Not always my strength. "I'll call him today or tomorrow."

Luke finishes his squats and steps out from the machine. As he walks by, he slaps my shoulder. "Good man. I've got to say, Leo, you really have been playing it smart lately."

I appreciate those words, and though I'm not looking forward to the call with my brother, I am excited to bring a gorgeous redhead breakfast in bed.

And I hope he's right. I abandoned one plan to hurt Carcetti, because it was too risky instead of just barreling ahead. Maybe this is all growth.

Then again, I don't have a new plan, and everyone knows Carcetti is about to make a move. Maybe old Leo had it right...

Workout done, I take the stairs two at a time. Stopping in the kitchen of my apartment, I pull out my blender and start mixing up a spinach smoothie. As hard as my workout is, dancing clearly zaps Kim of her energy, and she needs quality food.

She comes out of my room, wearing my T-shirt from the night before, her legs on full display, and I've got to be honest...the sight of her in my shirt does some weird shit to my insides.

She's so sexy and the fact that she's wrapped in my clothing, my scent, triggers some possessive instinct and has me moving around the island to pull her close.

"Tonight, bring an overnight bag to work."

"This is why you can't date your boss," she murmurs, but she still wraps her arms around my neck with a sleepy smile. "Bossy."

"Look," I'm already getting defensive. "We don't have to have sex, but I like what we did last night and—"

She squeezes my neck. "Any chance we could finish this discussion while we drink those smoothies you made? I'm starving and they look amazing."

I grin into her hair and then step away, filling two glasses. Handing one to Kim, I start to sip mine and look over in time to see hers is half gone.

I like a girl with an appetite, so I set mine down, and throw more banana and avocado into the blender.

She finishes one and I refill, pulling out a pan. "You need an egg."

She doesn't argue and I watch as Kim drinks the second smoothie and then eats two eggs. Silently, I pull out a grapefruit, slicing it up. Her eyes light up.

I make a note to order more groceries.

"Coffee?" I ask, going over to my espresso machine.

"No thank you. I don't drink much caffeine anyway and lately it smells funny…" She waves a hand, taking another slice of grapefruit. "This was really good. I can't afford groceries like this, and I think I actually feel better from eating so healthy, so I really appreciate it, Leo."

"You feel better from a smoothie?" A little alarm is sounding in the back of my thoughts.

"Maybe I have a vitamin deficiency or something."

I make a second note to call a doctor. My guess is it's been a while since she's had a check up.

"So…about the overnight bag?"

"Are you making me breakfast again?"

"Yep."

"Then I am in."

I smile as I finish my smoothie. "Now. How about a shower?"

"Gee. Let me think…" She taps her chin. "Six shower heads at your place or one really crappy one at mine…"

I pull her close. "You forgot about the automatic washer."

"Automatic washer?"

"Yeah. Me." I kiss her then, grapefruit on her lips. I bury a hand into the softness of her curls, pulling her belly tight to mine.

I love the way she fits into me. She kisses me several more times before she pulls away. "And a really great rinse cycle."

I laugh against her cheek. "This morning we might have to skip the rinse cycle but tonight..."

"Promises, promises," she murmurs against my skin as I pick her up, and carry her toward the bathroom.

I'm true to my word and we're in and out of the shower in under a half hour. She tosses on her clothes from the night before, while I put on my standard jeans and T-shirt and then we head down to the garage.

I start the car, shifting into reverse as the engine revs. "I've got to stop in a few other clubs. Why don't I leave you at your place and I'll be back to pick you up between two and three?"

"I don't want to be late. I'll get myself to work."

I grimace over at her. "I prefer driving you."

She touches my hand on the stick shift. "Thanks, Leo. But I don't want to be late. Everyone's been really nice, but—"

"Of course, they're nice. I have to hire nice people."

"Why's that?"

"Because I'm an asshole."

She shakes her head as a call comes in on my phone. My eyes flash to the screen and nearly bug out.

It's the New York Ballet.

In a quick move, I dismiss the call, Kim still fiddling with my hand. She didn't notice...my breath rushes out from my lungs. "You're not an asshole, you're just an alpha."

"How's that?" But I've never felt like more of a dick then I do in this moment.

"My last boyfriend cheated on me and then told me that it was because I was boring in bed. He's the asshole."

"Bobby said that to you?" Call forgotten, I think I might track Bobby down and punch him in the face.

I see her wince. "He also said that he'd thought a girl like me, no father figure, no money, would have had enough daddy issues to be good in bed."

"Fucker," I snarl. I can see her face is red with embarrassment, her eyes darting away. Bobby made a deep cut. Whatever else I do, I decide I'm healing that wound. I'm an asshole too, she just doesn't know it yet. But I'm an asshole who understands her worth, and at the very least, she'll understand that before this is all done.

"I shouldn't have told you. I don't know why I did."

"Yes, you should have." I hate thinking of her holding those feelings, what that douche bag said, inside.

"I never told anyone and I've worried—"

"He's not just an asshole, he's a manipulator, Kim. Don't listen to him." I slow the car as I pull up in front of her apartment. "Guys like that say a bunch of shit, not because it's true, but because they're hoping it will make you act the way they want you too."

Her eyes meet mine. "You don't think he's right? I've got no money. I can't even buy groceries."

I'm starting to understand why Kim's so worried about what other people think. "Sweetheart, I've got money, but my dad was a gangster. How does that make me better than you? I'm the one who should be worried about being trash."

She shakes her head. "But you run legit businesses. You're smart and successful."

I sigh. "I quit drinking because when I don't, I make better decisions. Mason is angry with me because I nearly really hurt him and Charlotte when I was on a bender. It was bad. I have some sins to atone for and some real actions that would cause people to think less of me." The very ones I'm trying to make up for. "But you, you don't."

She blinks at me, big green eyes, before she leans over and kisses me long and slow, holding my face like I just proved to her that Santa was real.

I want to sink into her. I want to say all the things that make her feel good. And then I want to make her feel even better by making her orgasm in every way possible.

"Leo," she whispers against my lips.

"Yeah, baby?"

"I don't want to masturbate tonight." She's still nibbling at my lip, her fingers digging into my neck.

"No?"

"I want to feel you inside me."

Fuck. I want that too. But I'm going to have to come clean about a few things too. And holy shit, is it going to suck.

CHAPTER FOURTEEN

KIM

I FINALLY LEAVE THE CAR, and to be honest, I feel better than I have in weeks. Between the night with Leo, solid sleep, and the amazing breakfast, I'm floating as I make my way up to my third-floor apartment.

Confessing a few of my fears to him wasn't so bad either. I've never had anyone other than Charlotte that not only accepted me for who I am, but actually made me feel better about myself.

I make a note to eat more spinach as I insert the key into my apartment door and walk inside.

Chandra and Kendall are sitting on the couch, each with a coffee in hand as I enter.

"Hey," I call out as I close the door and start for my room.

"Hey," Chandra calls from the seat. "Great job last night. You rocked the cages."

"Thanks," I say, continuing down the hall. After everything that happened last night, I just want some quiet time alone in my room. But Kendall jumps up, following.

"What kind of money did you make?" she says from behind me, and I know I'm not slipping away without being really rude. Which is tempting...

But I pause, partially turning. "Why?"

Chandra gets up too. "I heard some of the cage dancers say they can make close to a thousand a night if the tips are good."

"Yeah," I say, not sharing my specific pay, which was way more. Between the tips and the extra money Leo gave me, I've got more money than I've had in my entire life.

Kendall shifts. "Think I could get a job there?"

Kendall is a leggy brunette with solid dance skills, but she has a tendency to blow jobs up with her outrageous behavior. I've only been there a few days, but I've already heard that Leo keeps a strict behavior policy. I look at Chandra. "You ask?"

Chandra nods. "Mr. Kincaid didn't really answer but maybe if you asked...."

I give a little nod. I don't really like hitting Leo up for too many favors. I know he'd hire her if I asked, I sense it. But I'm also becoming more dependent on him in a way that makes me nervous. People I depend on don't exactly stick around in my life. "I'll ask."

Kendall gives me a relieved smile. "That's great. Thanks. With Danielle moving out..."

Chandra bumps Kendall, like she wasn't supposed to say anything. My stomach flutters with a bit of nerves. "Danielle's moving out?"

"Yeah," Chandra shrugs. "She got engaged and Dave doesn't like her living here. He wants her to move in with him."

I can imagine. Like I already mentioned, he's had to kick a few creeps out. "I'll talk to Leo today."

"Thanks," Kendall nods. "It would be great for all of us to make more money. Our lease is up next month."

Chandra gives Kendall another look. I'm not always the quickest with this stuff, but even I've scented the problem. We'll be three in a four-bedroom. "You guys don't want to stay here?"

Chandra is giving Kendall the shut-up face, that turns into a wince as she looks at me. "Well, you're leaving too, right? After Christmas?

And then it will just be me and Kendall. We don't really want two new roommates."

I stare at them, my mouth dropping open. Did Kendall just ask me to get her a better paying job so they can afford a place without me? "Did you two find a place already?" I ask it casually, but inwardly I'm freaking out. I just got my feet under me. I finally have a little money, and now I'm going to have no place to live? I cannot catch a break.

I swear, this is why I think I might be everything guys have lobbed at me the past few years. Trash. Hot mess. I can't seem to keep my life together for five minutes.

They both have the decency to look guilty. I turn, done with this conversation, as I start for my room again. "You'll still ask about the job, right?" Kendall calls.

"You're so stupid," I hear Chandra snark. "You weren't supposed to tell her."

I roll my eyes even as my stomach twists. What am I going to do? Sitting on my bed, my head hangs down. Why does everything have to turn to crap, the second one good thing happens?

My phone chimes and I look down to see Charlotte's name pop up on my screen. Crappy as today is, I smile to see her name.

She's asking me how I'm doing and without thinking, I text her what happened with Chandra and Kendall.

A second later, she calls. I pick up, determined to not weigh her down with my problems. "Hey, how's married life?"

"It's really good," I can hear her smile through the phone and I'm so happy for her. "But that's not why I called."

"Oh."

"I wanted to check on you and clearly my timing was spot on. I'm not surprised they are doing that to you. They were always bitches."

"Thanks," I whisper.

"I know the place is total crap, but I still have four months on my old lease if you need somewhere to crash."

I stare at the phone, relief making my shoulders limp. Charlotte had this tiny studio in a really shit neighborhood but it's like the answer to a prayer now. I could live alone and not go through all my money. Money I'll need for when I move. "Oh my God, you're serious? That would be amazing."

"I'm serious. Why don't we have lunch this week and I'll give you the keys?"

"Charlotte, seriously. Thank you."

"For you? Anything! I can't meet for lunch tomorrow but how about Saturday? Is that soon enough?"

"It's perfect." We talk for a few more minutes before I unpack my dance bag.

My money from last night is in there and I take it out, staring at the pile before I try to decide what to do with it.

I don't want to ask Leo too many favors, but as I hunt around my room, I'm not sure I want to leave it here either. I don't think Charlotte or Kendall would steal from me, but some of the guys they bring around might.

And I definitely don't want anything of value at Charlotte's place. There is a homeless encampment less than a block from her apartment and I know she had more than one break-in while she lived there.

Picking up my phone, I text Leo. I can't afford to let pride get in the way of my financial future.

Hey. Can I ask a favor?

He almost instantly replies back. *Anything, gorgeous.*

I smile as I type back. *Can I leave my cash at your place for now?*

Three dots appear and then very quickly. *Why, is something wrong?*

Two seconds later, another text appears. *Did one of your roommates steal from you?*

And then another. *Is there some dick at your place?*

I'm impressed he can type that fast as he sends one more. *I'm coming back.*

I STARE AT THE SCREEN, wondering what just happened. Finally, with a shake of my head. I type. *None of the above. No need to come back. Just thinking ahead.*

I DON'T HEAR anything from him and so, with a shrug, I put clean dance stuff and a few essentials in my bag, covering the money and then bring the bag to the bathroom with me to pack my toothbrush and my shampoo. Leo's stuff is really nice, but it smells like a guy's soap and shampoo. Then I plug in my straightener to do my hair.

But I'm only like a quarter of the way through when a knock sounds on the front door.

I ignore it, assuming that Chandra or Kendall has ordered food.

Until I hear Chandra trill a laugh. "Oh hey, Mr. Kincaid."

I set down the straightener and open the bathroom door. "Leo?"

He's marching down the hallway with his face set in hard lines, his eyes narrowed. "What's happened?"

I shake my head. "I told you. Nothing."

But Chandra is following, and she starts babbling in her Chandra way. "We're not kicking her out, we just—"

Leo pivots, his shoulders expanding, and I catch Chandra visibly start, I can just see her face over his shoulder. "What did you just say, Chandra?"

"Leo," I say, and now I sound angry. "It's fine." I stomp down the hall, tapping his shoulder.

I can see his profile and he is glaring at Chandra as she goes pale. Which is why I switch from tapping to smacking. I finally get his attention. I like that Leo's strong, I really do, but I don't need a neanderthal to fix my problems with my roommates. "What's she talking about?"

"Danielle got engaged, our lease is about to be up, and I'm moving to New York, so Kendall and Chandra are going to get a smaller place just the two of them."

"How soon?"

"Next month," Kendall volunteers. "And really nice to meet you. Chandra wasn't lying, you are really hot—"

It's my turn to glare. Kendall will sleep with almost anyone.

But Leo doesn't even look at her, he's staring at me. "You're not leaving Vegas until January."

"I talked with Charlotte. Her place—"

Leo's eyes narrow. "No fucking way. That place is a shithole."

My tongue clicks on the back of my teeth. "I'm not dancing at Temptation to spend all my money on rent. It defeats the purpose." My arms cross over my chest. "And you don't get to tell me no fucking way. I don't need a babysitter."

I've got Leo's full attention now and his features have gone black. "If I say you're not—" His voice is loud, but I ignore it. Men have scared me before, but not Leo. This is the man who gets down on his knees to give me pleasure. He washes me in the shower, and he makes me smoothies. He does not intimidate me.

"One more word in that tone and I'm not staying tonight." My arms cross over my chest.

His eyes widen as he takes a deep breath. I see him deflate and I silently marvel that I have that kind of power over him. "It's not safe there, baby, and I'd worry about you all the time if you stayed there."

Kendall and Chandra are watching and listening with rapt attention, and I know that they both caught the *baby* in that sentence.

But Leo is not looking at them at all, as he hooks my waist and pulls me close. "You can have one of the units in our building. There are several finished apartments that are empty. And I know you like the six-headed showers."

I shake my head, appreciating his suggestion far more than his dictate. "You know I can't afford a building like that." But my stomach is now pressed to his and both his arms are around me as my hands grasp his biceps.

"I'm not charging you. Don't be ridiculous."

"Oh my God," Kendall whispers. "I change my mind. I want to live with Kim."

"No," Leo answers for me, before he starts pulling me down the hall toward the front door. But I dig my heels, slamming on the breaks. I don't want to live with Kendall, but the problem with accepting Leo's charity is that he's now dictating who I room with. "I need to finish my hair."

"Finish it at the club."

"I'm not going out like this," I point at the one straight section with a bunch of curls around the rest of my head. "And I'll live where I want and with whom I choose." Then I push out of his arms.

"Kim," he says on a sigh, his fit of temper now gone. "It's just good sense to take me up on the offer."

"It's good safety," I correct. "But letting you tell me what to do might not be sensible."

He stares at me as I march back down the hall to the bathroom. "I can find my own way to work."

"No, I'll wait." And then he looks back at Kendall and Chandra with his lip curled like he hates the idea of having to make conversation with them. But I kind of marvel because I think I might have won this round, and I can't believe Leo would accede any of this to me.

Just before I close the bathroom door, I call out. "Kendall wants an interview." Privately, I know she won't be able to follow all Leo's rules and she'll likely be fired as quickly as she's hired.

But this isn't about Kendall. It's about Leo. I really like having him in my life but I'm not going to start letting him boss me around.

At least not in my own apartment.

That's the problem with sleeping with your boss. I wince as I close the bathroom door and start on my hair again.

It's the problem with never having a guy stick. Not even your own father. I don't trust any man with power over my life. So maybe Bobby was right about the daddy issues…

I know Leo and I are moving deeper into that grey area where the rules are unclear, but I can't seem to stop myself, and I'm not sure I want to.

When I come out of the bathroom, Leo is sitting on the couch staring daggers at Kendall and Chandra.

I sigh as I heave my bag up on my shoulder. "Ready."

He rises from the cushion, not saying a word as he comes to stand at my side. I nip at my lip as I look back at Kendall and Chandra.

Chandra gives me a wave as she winces while Kendall pushes up from her seat. "If you change your mind about the interview..."

Leo says nothing as he takes the bag from my shoulder. We walk out into the hall and down to his waiting car. I cannot believe he parked that car on my street, but I don't say anything, knowing I'm the one who made him leave it there for close to an hour.

It's not until he's slid into the driver's seat and starts the car that he speaks, "You are not rejecting my offer to come live in my building."

"You are not my boyfriend."

The words are out of my mouth before I can take them back. He slips on some aviator sunglasses—they look hot as hell, but do little to hide his glare. "What does that have to do with anything?"

My lips part. "You tried to tell me where I was living and who I could live with."

He aggressively shifts the car, punching the accelerator. "That Kendall is bad news. Chandra's OK, but Kendall..."

"I know," I rub my temples. "Just like I know that Charlotte's place is a safety nightmare. The point is that we are not some unit, where you make decisions for me, Leo. When you're gone from my life, I have to live with wherever I am at when you exit."

He shifts again. "We're both going to think like Mason for a second."

I don't really like those words. Does Leo think he's less than his brother? I like Mason and all, but he's a bit cold for me. I know Leo's got a temper, but I also feel deep in my gut that with him, I'm safe when we're together. He's got this warmth that makes me feel...

I leave that thought as Leo continues. "Mason would say that living rent-free would only give you more options. And that pride shouldn't get in the way of sound financial decisions."

I harrumph. "I don't know about Mason, but Leo is giving some sound advice."

That earns me a half smile, the crock of his mouth only making him more gorgeous.

"What I don't appreciate is you giving me orders."

His smile disappears.

"I might be doing a shitty job of running my life, but I have been running it. And believe it or not, some of my principles do keep me from hating myself or getting in trouble. I don't take charity because men who give it, they frequently have an ulterior motive."

He slows down to take a right, his lips pressed into a hard line. "That is a really good point. And I'm sorry that I sounded like I was giving you orders."

He pulls the car over in front of a club I've never been to before and turns toward me in his seat. "I promise there won't be any strings attached if you come live in the building. Or maybe, Mason has another building, because the Italians bombed the one I live in a few months back. If we're talking safety…"

"Did you say it was bombed?" These are not words one expects to hear, and I think back to his comment about his dad being a gangster. Apparently, he meant legitimate gangster and some details about the power these men carry themselves with makes more sense. They do things other men would not. That's why they feel deep-down alpha.

And for some reason, that doesn't scare me. In fact, it makes me feel safe.

He sighs. "Yeah. I put the Italians' favorite hitman behind bars. Now both Toni Carcetti and his nephew Little Anthony Carcetti want revenge."

"I'm trying to keep up here. Bombed? Revenge?"

"It's why Charlotte and Mason moved. And if I'm honest, Mason might not want you there and neither do I. I'll see what I can work out."

I shake my head. "Leo…"

"I know. I'm trouble. I get it." He takes off his sunglasses, his eyes meeting mine. "But that doesn't mean I can't put you in a better place, Kim. Because what I do have is money and real estate. Take advantage, Kim. I won't ask too much and you might be my chance to leave someone better than when I found them. That's what I'm trying for here."

I give a tentative nod. Because...those words make me even warmer.

He relaxes as he runs a hand through his hair. "I'm not trying to control you and I won't ask anything from you. But I meant what I said, Kim. Even after...if you need anything, you come to me. Or if I'm not around, you go to Mason. I promise you, my brother would give you anything you want, with no strings other than being nice to Charlotte."

Leo really knows how make a girl's panties melt. He gets out of the car and comes around to my side of the door. I guess it's "bring your sex buddy to work" day. I know we're moving into deeper and darker waters, but I can't seem to stop myself, as I slip my hand in his.

CHAPTER FIFTEEN

Leo

I look over a row of columns in the accounting books for Regal, one of our smaller clubs, as Kim lounges on the settee in my office. It's only been a few hours since I came all over her stomach, and yet, I'd love nothing more than to bend her over that little couch and fuck her every which way.

She's laying on her side, typing something into her phone, the position highlighting the curves of her body.

I look down again, realizing I've completely lost my place. At this rate, we're never going to make it back to Temptation.

But before I can really start again, my phone buzzes, Mason's number flashing on my screen.

He hasn't called in a while, and as my gaze flicks back to Kim, I don't have to wonder what this is about. I'm sure my conversation with the other Kincaids has gotten back to Mason. "Hello?"

"Got a minute?"

"Yeah. Just give me a sec, Mason." I give Kim a quick smile and then get up from the desk, as she sits up and gives me a questioning stare.

I wink and then cross the room to kiss her temple before I step out of the office and down the hall to the empty locker room.

"What's up?" I finally ask, ready for whatever's coming my way.

"I need to talk to you about Kim," Mason says, his tone giving nothing away.

At least he's direct. I appreciate that. "Sure."

"I hear you hired her."

"I did." I'm walking back and forth to expel extra energy. I didn't used to be so twitchy. I've always liked being physical, maybe more than any of my brothers. But after my father was shot, it was like I was consumed by anger.

"And that she's killing it at Temptation."

"She is." I stop in front of a mirror, noting the lines of tension around my mouth and eyes. I'm not sure where Mason is taking this.

Mason pauses. "And that her roommates are bailing on her."

"Charlotte told you."

Mason lets out a long breath. "Is something going on between you and Kim?"

Old Leo would have told him to fuck off and stay out of my business.

"Listen, Mason."

"I'm listening and you better make this good," he grits into the phone.

Fuck. You. But I hold the words in, drawing in several deep breaths before I actually speak. "Whatever you're worried about, I've got her making mad money at Temptation, I'm there every night she is, and I will not allow her to move into Charlotte's old place. There is no reason she should be in a hellhole like that when we've got more real estate than we know what to do with."

Mason is silent for so long, I wonder if he hung up on me. Finally, he speaks, "Are you thinking of moving her into the building you're living in with the guys?" he asks. His change in mood and tone catch me off guard, but I recover quickly.

"No. The Italians are more of a threat than ever, and we both know that the Carcettis are gearing up for some big move. I don't think it's safe enough there."

"Agreed," Mason rumbles.

Mason and I never agree. Never. "For that reason, I think a different building would be better. Got anything else I can move us into?"

"Us?" Mason asks, his voice sharp.

"I wouldn't want her in a building alone either."

"Roman could—"

"Fuck that." I know I didn't directly answer his question about my relationship with Kim, but we both know what's happening here. Still, this moment should be about reason, not about me acting like a blunt hammer. I might actually be learning a few things here. "With her working at Temptation, I've been driving her back and forth. The nights are late. I'm a better choice than Roman, since I can also act as chauffeur."

"I agree." I blink twice, surprised Mason is being so…reasonable. All Kincaids have a hard head and when it comes to me and him…

"I've actually got another building I just finished. It's empty but the penthouse is gorgeous. Maybe you should take her there."

I stare at my phone. What is happening? My brother is supporting my ideas? "Okay."

"Jake says that you're doing really well with staying sober."

"Mason, you're officially being weird."

He chuckles. "Yeah. Probably. But I can hear that you're way more worried about Kim's safety and future than your own agenda, and that helps. I'm proud of you."

"I don't need your pride," I bite back, sounding like old Leo. Because he's hit a sore spot. I did do something completely selfish where Kim is concerned.

And I deserve Mason's irritation. I scrub a hand down my face. I'm the reason that Kim didn't get the spot at the New York Ballet. She was their first choice, but I made a generous donation for them *not* to hire her until the winter. That way she'd stay in Vegas a little longer.

I know it was a shit thing to do. I wanted her in my bed again. I had rationalized that once we'd had some more time together, I'd call the ballet and have them invite her back. But as I think about it, I know it's one of those types of choices that caused me a great deal of problems in the past and I shouldn't have done it.

"There is no need to be angry," he rumbles, not sounding irritated. "But if compliments bother you, can we talk about the apartment at least?"

I know Mason is trying. More than I am, and it's not his fault I did something completely dickish. Something I have to confess to her soon. But I focus on Mason now. "Yeah. That would be great." And speaking of confessing. "But first, I'm not going to lie to you, I don't really do long-term, but I plan on helping Kim get to New York safely and with plenty of money in her pocket."

Mason lets out another long breath. "I don't love the idea of you and her, but Charlotte says that Kim is a big girl who can do what she wants."

"She is that. Doesn't take much shit either..."

Mason laughs again, "Charlotte also said that Kim doesn't date unless she really wants to. And..." Mason scrubs his jaw, I hear it. "And I can tell that you are taking her safety seriously, which I really appreciate."

I hang up, kind of irritated. I could hear that Mason was leaving out the topic of me and Kim dating because Charlotte was making him. But if he had his druthers...Mason would be all up in my grill. Hence my irritation. Well that, and Mason does that to me. I know he means well, but he's a bossy prick and I'm not a man who wants to be bossed.

But I can't deny my brother is really smart, and he's got a good head for planning. For the first time since I hatched this Toni Carcetti plan, I consider asking his opinion. I can be the instrument that brings justice but maybe with Mason involved, I could do it discreetly, without landing myself in prison.

Mason and I really are mending some fences... though he still pisses me off.

Returning to the office, however, I forget all about my brother when I find Kim stretched out on her back, her pretty feet dangling off one end of the couch.

I lean over, kissing her lips as she winds her arms around my neck. "Everything all right?"

"Fine." I kiss her again. "Mason has another building he thinks we should move into."

Her brows lift. "Mason is suggesting that both you and I move into some building together?"

"Mason wants you safe. And though he doesn't approve of much of what I do, maybe rightfully so, he's all for you living in a decent apartment."

"There is no way that the apartment is 'decent.' It's sure to be downright decadent."

That makes me laugh. "You've got me there."

"You and Mason aren't getting along so well?"

"He thinks he is my keeper. I don't like being kept." Then I shake my head. "And like I said, I fucked up."

She nods. "I remember."

"So I'm trying to prove that I deserve his trust again. That's how you right a wrong, correct?"

"Yes. That's how."

"I honestly thought he was going to roast me for getting involved with you." My fingers slide into her hair, unable to keep from touching more of her.

"But he thinks you have good intentions like helping me pay tuition and keeping me from really awful neighborhoods."

"Yeah. About that and my good intentions. That night we hooked up at the wedding—"

A knock interrupts us. "Mr. Kincaid," the manager of Regal calls. "Can I have your assistance at the bar?"

"Go," Kim whispers. "I'm going to sign up for my class."

I get up, reluctantly leaving her side as I head out to the bar. This conversation is to be continued.

CHAPTER SIXTEEN

Kim

We make it to Temptation and I'm only a few minutes late, not that anyone says a word when I walk through the back with Leo.

Everyone seems to understand that Leo and I are… something. I thought they might care but everyone is super nice to me.

Maybe they think we were already seeing each other and not that I started to sleep with the boss to get special treatment?

I don't worry about it as the other dancers and I rehearse, grab a bite, and then relax before we start changing for the night.

I might have to talk to Leo about a second uniform. And I'm not taking advantage, but the full suit is really hot, even with the air vents, and I know if I say I'm uncomfortable he'll get me something different.

Leo is not my boyfriend.

I said it today and he didn't disagree. Not that I'm surprised. I knew who he was when I started this.

But he's done a better job than any other man I've ever met at taking care of me when I really needed it and I'm so grateful.

The problem for me is that I'm starting to develop real feelings.

I hit the platform, the crowd already primed and roaring as the cages start up from the floor.

I don't have to see Leo to know he's here watching.

It makes me more confident and as I start the set, I know I'm dancing for him. I'm bolder, more amped, and the club responds, the flood lights pointed at me as I dip and turn.

When the first break comes, I'm not even close to tired and I hit the platform already antsy to dance again.

I have to conserve energy, I know that.

But I also know that the tips are going to be really good tonight. It's such a nice change.

Melissa is off to one side of the platform. She's been watching me all night and I have no idea why. She doesn't seem jealous. Maybe she's just worried about the boss being with the one of the dancers? But her attention has been weird. "You've gotten called down by security. Mr. Kincaid must want to see you," she calls to me. "If you're not back in time, I'll put someone in your cage."

I shake my head, starting down the stairs in my three-inch heels. I'm not sure I'll ever get used to the preferential treatment. Clearly, she's not too worried about me and Leo if she's offering to cover for me. So what's her deal?

I make it to the back hall that doesn't usually allow foot traffic, but there is a man in the hall. He's dressed in a cheap suit, his dark hair slicked back and a toothpick hanging out of his mouth. Our eyes meet and my breath stills.

If Leo doesn't frighten me no matter what he does, this man scares the shit out of me with just a glance. It's something in his eyes...

They are snakelike in their assessment, his lip curling as his gaze slides down my body. "So you're Kim—"

But a random group of four guys enters the hall. Scary man looks back at them and then veers off to the back door of the club. Is he a Kincaid I haven't met? I'm watching him leave, not paying attention to the other men until I hear my name. "Kim?"

I turn my head then stop short.

It's my ex-boyfriend. My stomach drops out as dread fills my limbs. "Bobby?"

"Actually, I go by Robert now," he smiles at me, stopping just in front of me. He's broader than I remember but no less smarmy.

He's still handsome with classic features and a good jaw. But he's sporting a fake tan, it's too even, and frosted tips. Why didn't I see that when we dated? He's got fake written all over him.

"Well, Robert, it's good to see you but I've got to go. My boss is—"

I try to pass him, but his hand shoots out, grabbing my arm. "Kim. Wait."

I don't like him touching me and I try to scoot away but his hand tightens. "Let me go, all right? Like I said, I'm working and—"

"Oh, I saw you," he murmurs in this intimate way I don't like at all as he leans close. "How come you were never like that when we were dating?"

My lip curls. Who asks that? Leo's words are echoing in my head about how Bobby is just a manipulative asshole. I think Leo is right.

I try to jerk away, wanting to get to Leo's office and end this painful conversation.

Bobby's hand bites into me instead of letting me go, as he pulls me close, his lips pressing to my ear. "I always knew you were a slut underneath that cold exterior—"

I take my heel, the three-inch spike, and lift it up, kicking out, raking it down his shin.

He loosens his grip, I hear his crying grunt of pain as I spin away, bouncing off the wall before I try to move down the hall.

But he recovers and grabs me again and this time his touch is really rough as his fingers bite into my biceps, probably leaving bruises. He yanks me and I half fall against him. "See, I knew you were hot even if you played frigid."

"Fuck you," I spit back, even as tears sting at my eyes. "If I was frigid, it's because I knew that under your nice-guy act is a complete jerk."

"You want to fuck me?" he's pulling me roughly against him, his friends forming a circle around us that blocks me from view. Now, I'm really getting scared as I try to scream.

But his hand presses hard over my lips, his eyes mean and angry. "I treated you like a girlfriend when I should have..."

But he doesn't finish as one of his friends flies across the hall, crashing into the far wall.

I stare, not sure what happened, when Leo's face appears between me and Bobby. "One more word out of your stupid fucking mouth and they are going to find your body torn apart in the desert and picked over by the buzzards," Leo snarls.

I go limp with relief as Bobby turns toward Leo. "I don't know who the fuck you think you are, buddy, but why don't you mind your own business?"

"See, that was like fifteen words," Leo says with a lethal smile that might make another person's blood run cold. I've never been so happy to see anything in my life.

And then he grabs Bobby by the neck, yanking him away from me like my ex is a rag doll and not a man who is nearly six feet tall and at least one hundred eighty pounds. Leo's got him up on his tiptoes with only one hand as he snarls in Bobby's face.

"You know who I am, sunshine?" He gives Bobby a rough shake. I swear, I hear Bobby's teeth rattle. "I'm the man who kicks your fucking ass."

"Holy shit," one of the friends points at Leo. "You're a Kincaid."

"I'm a Kincaid," he answers. He's practically spitting in Bobby's face. "I eat stupid frat boys like you for breakfast."

I'm still against the wall and I haven't said a word. I don't want to make it worse but also...my legs are jelly.

He pulls Bobby back and then pops him in the nose with a single punch. It doesn't even look that hard but it's like Leo opened a floodgate, Bobby's nose starts gushing blood as he lets out a scream.

Leo drops him then as I start sinking down the wall. He's next to me in a second, pulling my body against his, lifting me in his strong arms.

I wrap my arms about his neck, a clear view of Bobby on the ground as Leo carries me away.

A little sob escapes my lips, my body jerking with the cry. Leo only wraps me tighter in his arms. "You're safe, sweetheart. Don't worry. I'd never let a scumbag like that hurt you."

A few tears leak out of my eyes. "I thought..."

One of his hands come to the back of my neck while the other is still wrapped around my thighs as he cradles me. "Don't think. Not now. Just put your weight on me and know that you're safe, that I'm here, and that I'm not going to let anyone hurt you."

I do exactly as he commands, not even paying attention to where he's carrying me until he knocks on a door.

That's when I realize he's taken me to the locker room.

Several of the dancers are still there, all of them staring at us with big eyes as Leo goes in, grabs my bag from my locker, and leaves again, never setting me down. I don't even have time to wonder what they might think...

Because Leo carries me straight out the back door to his car.

"Leo," that finally pulls me from my stupor. "I need to dance, I..."

But he just scowls. "You need a hot bath. I'm taking you home."

And then he opens the car door and sets me down in the bucket seat. How does he carry me so easily, setting me in his low-slung car? He hunches in with me, doing up my seatbelt.

He closes my door leaving me alone for a few seconds as he comes round the car, and that's when my thoughts snap back to his words. Home? I'm not even sure I have one of those. Then again, I know wherever Leo is taking me, if he's there, it's probably going to feel a lot more like a home than any other place I've been in the last four years.

CHAPTER SEVENTEEN

Leo

Kim is slumped in the seat next to me, her eyes closed. Inside I'm hectic, but I'm trying to keep it cool for her sake. Still, every time I think of that man's hands on her…

I grip the steering wheel tighter, my knuckles turning white. I've never allowed myself to be attached to anyone but family. Relationships are complicated, even more so for me.

And I never intended to have a woman to care for. Hell, I can barely take care of myself. Three weeks ago, I fully expected to rot in prison. Which is why I have no intention of adding labels to what we're doing.

But Kim is spectacular and there is bound to be other men who wish to claim her. I punch the car into fifth gear, my teeth grinding together.

The idea of someone else dating her makes me crazy.

The idea of one of them hurting her? That makes me murderous.

The feeling that I am her protector, that it's my job, my most important function to keep her safe, washes through me.

It's been there all along. The need to hire her, give her money, provide her with a nice, safe place to live. I've been acting as her protector almost from the first. Maybe even that call from the ballet…

Then again, I don't get to excuse the guilt on that one.

"You're going ninety," she murmurs.

I downshift, slowing the car down. So much for being a good protector. "That guy really pissed me off."

"I thought so, the blood gushing from his nose clued me in." And then she smiles.

I smile too. "I didn't scare you, did I, baby?"

She turns to look at me. "Scare me, Mr. Kincaid? No. You didn't scare me."

Calling me by the boss's name unleashes something feral in me. That's for people I don't eat out while kneeling in front of them. "I told you I'd put you over my knee if you called me that. If it were any other night, I just might."

"I think a spanking from you sounds totally hot, but I honestly don't think you'd enjoy giving it to me."

"What makes you say that?" I like kink as much as the next guy. Maybe more.

"You seem way more into making me feel good."

That was totally true. "You're not wrong," I grunt.

"Which is why, I'm hoping you'll put me on your body instead."

God, I want that so bad. "It's been a long night, baby. I don't want to scare you. Honestly, tonight seems like a good night for snuggling."

"Leo," she reaches across the console, her hand tracing up my inner thigh. "Remember that time we hooked up at your brother's wedding?"

My brows lift. "Vividly."

"You've made me feel safe from that moment to this one. I've never let so many of my inhibitions fall away…" She trails off, her hand stopping just against my ball sack in my jeans.

I punch the accelerator again, just wanting to get her home, I mean, back to my apartment, and get her clothes off.

I'm still starting us in the bath. I've got a nice large soaking tub and

I'm going to wash every one of that asswipe's touches away. And then I'm going to put her on top of me and let her ride me however she wants.

Because I've tried to dominate my entire life, but with Kim… I want whatever she wants. I want her to feel good and when it comes to her pleasure…

I just want to be her slave.

She was absolutely right about that and it's the strangest thing.

"I think we should do some furniture shopping tomorrow."

"Furniture shopping?" she sits up then.

"For the new place."

"Wait…my new place or your new place?"

That is an excellent question and for some reason, when Mason mentioned a penthouse, I just assumed it would be for two. Why would she sleep anywhere else besides my bed?

The building comes into view, and I hit the button for the gates, which open just long enough for my car to pull in and then they clank closed again.

I meant what I said about not doing long-term, but living with Kim until she leaves for the east coast isn't exactly long-term.

Then again, it's way longer than any other relationship I've ever been in. And what's even stranger is the more time that goes by, the more I seem to want Kim.

I thought after the wedding, if I could just have her a few more times, this attraction would burn out. But it only seems to be getting hotter.

Instead of feeling satiated, I'm hungrier than ever…

I park the car, barely shutting it off, before I'm out of the driver's seat and coming around the back bumper to open her door.

I help her out, pulling her into my side as I hustle her to the elevator. I can't explain why I'm frantic, but I just want her tucked in my room, in my bed, where I know she'll be safe and warm.

Of course, she'll likely have my cock inside her.

We get into the elevator and as the doors close, I'm lifting her in my arms, but unlike the last time when I pressed her against the wall, this time, I just drop my head into her neck, breathing in her scent.

I must be coming down from the adrenaline, because I think about what happened, and a few questions start swirling. "Why did you come downstairs during your set?"

"You called," she answers automatically.

"I did not."

She stiffens in my arms. "But Melissa said…."

"Melissa? That's weird… I'll talk to her about it tomorrow." It's a fact I file away for later.

The elevator stops and the doors slide open. I drop her bag in the entry and then carry Kim straight to the bathroom. I want to touch her skin, check her and make sure she isn't too hurt.

She's still in her full leather suit and I set her down on the tile floor, starting to work the zipper and help her out of it, which basically means peeling it off her.

She kicks off her heels, sighing.

When we've freed her torso, I cross to the tub, sitting on the edge to turn on the taps. I look back just in time to see her wiggling her hips out of the skintight cloth.

A rumble fills my chest as I tug my shirt over my head. I kick off my shoes just in time for her to pull her second leg out of the leather so that she's in nothing but a thong. Her back is to me, but Kim doesn't have a bad side and I'm devouring the curve of her back, her perfect ass. My gaze skims down her long, lean legs and then back up her body, mapping every little freckle as she tosses the suit to the side.

I reach out, grasping her waist and sliding my hands down her hips. She smiles at me over her shoulder as I pull her into my body.

She's still looking at me as I bring my hands to her stomach and then skim them up to cup her breasts.

I feel her gasp, her nipples peaking in my palms as she pushes up on tiptoe, but she doesn't kiss me.

Instead, she rubs the tip of her nose against mine. "Leo."

Something in the tone of it makes my breath hold in my chest. It's sweet and vulnerable and needy. "Baby."

"I know how much you've done for me. I'll pay you back someday. Promise."

She's got this ridiculous sense of fair. I've never met someone more concerned with not taking, despite how little she has, and it makes it so easy to give. I can be stingy but not with her. Never with her. I let go of one of her tits to run my palm back down her belly and then I slide my fingers into her thong, my middle finger gliding right through her folds. "You give me more than enough."

"I don't give you anything," she whispers.

I kiss her then, her sweet mouth so soft under mine. One of my hands is tweaking a nipple, the other is cupping her pussy while my finger circles her clit. Her hips are starting to move, chasing the pleasure, as she bucks into my palm.

I don't even know how to explain to her that I don't need her to give me anything other than permission to let me keep her close.

It's my job to give to her. Care for her. It's her job to...

I guess I see the problem. She must not think sex is enough. But for me, it is. She steals my breath every time I look at her and the fact I get to touch her...

"You give me plenty." And then I push my fingers lower, one of them sliding into her soaking wet pussy.

We both groan, and I look back to realize the tub is about to overflow.

Reluctantly, I let her go, sliding my hand back out of her underwear. I turn off the water and then drain some so that we don't overflow it. She's taking off her thong and I reach out my hand to help her into the tub.

She steps in, sinking into the water with a sigh, as I shuck off my jeans to climb in behind her. Her skin slides against mine as she settles back into me. I reach for some soap and start scrubbing her down.

I mostly just want to touch her skin. There are some faint bruises on her biceps but that's about it. My fingers glide over them as I kiss her neck, her ear. I hate that he left them on her, and I do my best to soothe them away.

But I'm no longer in a hurry. Now that we're naked, I honestly want to slow this down. I've never been a guy for taking my time. I like things fast and hot. But tonight, right now, I feel different.

Like it's more important to be slow and gentle. To show her… I search for the words.

To show her that she's in good hands.

I try not to think about why that's important to me. My hands are gliding over her belly, her body relaxing into mine as I kiss along her shoulder. She reaches back and twines her fingers into my hair.

Which means, I scrub the soap across her exposed armpit, making her jerk her arm away with a wild giggle.

"Are you ticklish?" I'm grinning too, wanting to touch her there again. Maybe I want to tickle her there with the stubble on my chin.

"No," she gasps, moving away to give me a little splash.

I love knowing this about her and I pull her close again turning her upper half so that her breasts are crushed into my chest, her hip pressing into my groin.

Her arms twine around my neck as I kiss her, sliding my tongue into her mouth to really taste her.

The tub is big but not big enough that she could straddle me that way I'd like her to, so I push up, holding her waist as I rise, water cascading down our bodies. I step out of the tub, carrying her with me. Water spills onto the floor as I grab a towel. I don't want to stop kissing her long enough to dry off, so instead, I heave her higher, my arm under her ass so that her legs wrap around me.

Which has my cock pushing against her pussy.

I slide in slowly, remembering how tight she was last time. It's not different this time, her walls gripping me as I ease in.

But she doesn't seem nervous tonight.

In fact, her hips arch in a way that pulls me in deeper. It looks so beautiful, the way her body rolls but it feels even better. "My little dancer," I grit out, pushing deeper inside her. I'm half tempted to just fuck her right here. The floor is slippery though, the pools of water on the marble. And I want to see her ride me, watch her hips roll, and so I start for the bedroom door, keeping my cock buried deep as I hold both her ass cheeks in my hands. Even as I walk, I'm naturally pumping in and out of her, her little whimpers and mewls making my cock harder as I walk and fuck her at the same time.

Sex with Kim is on some other level. She grips me with her legs, leaning her upper body away from me which drives me even deeper inside her.

I stop walking, my vision blurring. It's so good, I can't even breathe, so instead, I just hold her ass as tightly as I can.

She squirms, creating all sorts of feels before I finally release some of the pressure so she can bounce on my cock again.

It's so good, I stand next to the bed, just letting her ride me like this until I remember…I want more visuals.

Falling back on the bed, she lands on top of me. Instantly, she pushes up on my chest, so that her hips rock my cock deep inside her. I gnash my teeth together, a greedy snarl of pleasure pulling from my lips.

But she isn't done. With a gorgeous roll, she starts riding me. Just like her dancing, her body is fluid, beautiful, her tight sheath rubbing up and down my cock making my balls so tight, I think they might burst.

But I'm not cumming yet.

My girl needs to break first. Her eyes are glazed and unfocused, these needy little moans falling from her lips as she moves faster and faster. Soon her moans become a keening cry that has me grunting in response, words totally failing me.

That's when I grab her hips in my hands and pull her tighter into my pelvis, giving her clit what it craves.

She screams out my name, finally breaking, her movements fast and jerky, the rhythm gone as she rides out her pleasure. I love it so much, it sets off my own orgasm, as I pump her full of my cum, my guttural grunts joining hers.

She rides me until she seeks out every last bit of pleasure and then she collapses on my chest. "That was…"

I know. Holding her to my chest, I roll her over so she's under me now. Her body is soft and pliant as she tosses her hands above her head, her face falling to one side. I kiss a trail along her neck wanting even more of her taste on my tongue.

My cock starts to stir again, which surprises even me. I just came.

She lets out a sleepy little sigh, the fingers in one of her hands twining in mine. I feel the moment she relaxes into sleep, and I lift my head. Our feet are still dangling over the side and my cock is pressing into her soaking wet folds. "Kim?"

"Mmhmm," she murmurs as she bends one of her legs around mine, and then wraps my calf with hers. It's intimate and hot all at the same time. "You're hard again."

She's so pliant in my arms. "You do that to me, baby."

She smiles, her eyes still closed, even as her other leg hooks about my waist.

The invitation is clear.

"You sure you're up for another round?" I whisper into her skin.

"You feel so good, Leo," she sighs out. "Fuck me again."

She doesn't have to ask me twice. I thrust inside her, deep and hard. In the tub, I wanted her to know she was cherished.

But now...I want her to know she's mine.

CHAPTER EIGHTEEN

Kim

Leo thrusts into me like a man who's been starved. We haven't had sex in a while, but there have been plenty of orgasms, and I'm honestly taken aback by his need until the head of his cock hits the spot deep inside that sends my back arching, my body chasing more of what he gives.

It's fast and it's hard and it feels so good that I don't even realize I'm begging out loud for him to give me more, to give it to me harder, until he's spitting in my ear. "I will always give you what you need."

He's just making sexy talk. I know that.

But the promise still sets off some super button in my girl brain and with my arms tight about his neck, I start begging louder. "I know. That's it. Just like that. Oh God..."

"You like it when I fuck you hard, don't you, baby?"

"Yeah," the word comes out in a broken gasp, my body so on fire, I can barely make my throat work.

I absolutely break apart, screaming out my finish until my eyes are rolling back in my head and stars blur my vision.

It's like nothing I've felt before and I can barely breathe as he cums too, his body shuddering out his orgasm.

I'm limp underneath him, completely spent. And as amazing as that was, I don't think I can handle a third round.

My eyes close and I swear, I'm falling asleep seconds after.

"And they say guys conk out after sex." He's laughing in my ear as he lifts me up and pulls the covers back, sliding me into place in the bed.

I smile even as he gets up and goes back to the bathroom, bringing out a wet cloth and wiping me down.

I have to giggle a little because I just got out of the bath and I'm already a mess again. But it's the best kind of mess. Done, he cleans himself up too and then climbs into the bed next to me.

"Tomorrow, we've got to discuss birth control if we're going to be doing this on the regular."

Birth control! The word rockets through me and my eyes fly open. Why has this not occurred to me before right this second?

We haven't used birth control. I was militant with my last relationship, so I have no idea why protection has slipped my mind. I've let Leo cum in me multiple times without a thought to the potential consequences.

At least not this type. It's just that things with Leo got so hot and I got so caught up...

Mentally, I start counting back. When was the last time I had my period? As a dancer, I'm less regular than a lot of girls but...

I sit up, clutching the covers to my chest.

"What's wrong?" Leo asks, his brow scrunched as I stare at him.

"We...we didn't use anything that first time at Mason and Charlotte's wedding." I can hear the tremble in my voice. I've been off the past few weeks. Hungry, tired, nauseous with vertigo. I start to sweat, my head swimming.

He cocks a brow with a half smile. "It was a little last minute and pretty fucking fast," but then his smile dies as his gaze sweeps over me. "Kim. Are you okay?"

I shake my head. "Leo. We didn't use anything six weeks ago. I..."

Some understanding dawns in his eyes as his brow turns down into an angry slash. "You can't be serious."

I'm shaking as I clutch the covers. "I don't know. I mean I don't always get my period but…"

"Fuck," he yells out and he's out of the bed, standing naked in front of me with his hands on his hips. "Do not do that girl thing where you decide it would be fun to fuck with me—"

My mouth opens and closes, words failing me, because when have I ever done that? And where is this coming from? It hurts that he'd even accuse me of girl drama.

He's pacing now, his movements jerky and agitated as he runs his hands through his hair. His features are taut and there is this storm in his eyes that makes me curl into myself. For the first time since I met Leo, I'm scared.

Maybe not of him, but of how this is going to go down. "Leo." I sound weak. I'm not the same woman who told him he couldn't boss me around this morning. I feel it…this could be the end of everything. With him. But with my life too. I'm wilting.

"I should know better than to let some random chick convince me to fuck her at a wedding of all places."

Those words trigger something inside me. I seduced him? I know where this is going.… I'm just that girl who is promiscuous enough to lead some good boy astray. That puts some fight back in me and I cling to it. "You convinced me!" I cry out. I surge up on my knees, letting the blanket fall away.

"This is so typical." He says it loud. Not yelling but close. "How the hell could you let this happen? I can't fucking believe I trusted—"

"What?" I cut him off because those words are like a punch to the gut. "Don't you dare accuse me of being some money-grubbing whore or some trashy—" But I can't go on. Because I just realized...

It's happening. The very thing that happened to my mother.

The thing I've been fighting to avoid. I wasn't going to be some single mom. She gave up her dreams for me, but I was going to live those dreams for both of us.

My knees give out as I collapse back onto the bed. I cover my face with my hands, burying my head in the pillow because I am, in fact, the trashy slut who let some guy knock her up on a one-night stand. I hate myself so much in this moment as I curl into a ball and let out a feral cry.

I've done the one thing I've promised myself I wouldn't do. All those dates I didn't go on in high school and college. My one boyfriend, the guy I thought would be safe.

I've thrown it all away, and all because one guy convinced me to really let loose.

What is my mom going to say? How am I going to live with myself? I need to get out of here. I scrub my hands over my face. "Where's my bag?"

"What?" Leo asks and he doesn't sound angry anymore. The word is cautious. Maybe even afraid as he touches my shoulder.

"I've got to go. Where is my bag?"

"You can't leave now. It's the middle of the night."

"I'm not your problem. This is not your problem," I say as I shrink away, tears sliding down my face. "My bag. Is it in the bathroom? The car?" I surge up. I've got to find it, get some real clothes, and leave.

I can't do this. I can't.

But I must have moved too fast because my head swims and then my stomach rolls.

Instead of searching, I surge out of the bed and toward the bathroom.

I only just make it when the contents of my stomach heave up my throat and into the toilet.

I don't even have it in me to fight when Leo's arm comes around me to support my weight, his other hand gathering up my hair to keep it clean.

I vomit until I'm empty in every way. I don't even feel tired. I swear, I feel nothing.

We're both naked. I have no idea how long I'm suspended over the toilet before he lifts me into his arms. He carries me back to the bed and I don't even protest as he lays me back.

I know I should leave but I don't think I can. I'm devoid of energy, of fight, as I lay exactly where he leaves me. He comes back and pulls me back up, pressing a glass to my lips.

I drink automatically but as a bit of water spills down my chin, that's when I realize that it's also coating my cheeks. How long have I been crying?

Leo's sets down the glass and then his large hand swipes over my face. "Kim." His voice is soft. Gentle.

But I don't respond. My eyes squeeze shut. "You can say it."

"Say what?"

"That you never want to see me again. That you think I'm some—"

"Do not say those things about yourself." His voice is back to having a hard edge and it actually makes me feel better, like things are less strange. But they aren't right… they'll never be right again. My whole life is changing because I couldn't keep my legs closed.

My lips press shut as I close my eyes. "You were going to say them before. I could hear it in your voice."

"I wasn't going to call you any names and besides, we both know I'm an ass. I got scared, that's all."

"I'm scared too." The words shiver through me.

"Look. We don't know anything. Let's get some sleep and then we can figure this out in the morning."

I nod because it makes sense and because there is nothing else to do.

Leo climbs in the bed and holds me close, but it doesn't feel the same.

I'm pretty sure whatever delusional bubble I've been living in just burst.

Still, he tries. "I promised you that I would always keep you safe, Kim. And that's what I intend to do."

CHAPTER NINETEEN

Leo

Kim falls asleep but I'm crawling out of my skin. So when I know she's deep asleep, I climb from the bed and head out to the living room.

I grab my briefs on the way out, pulling them on. I don't turn on a light. Instead, I move to the windows and stare out at the Las Vegas skyline.

This fucking place. It's so easy to fall into sin here. Look at my parents. My mother died in a car crash in one of her alcoholic stupors.

And my father...

I move into the kitchen, opening the cupboard above the refrigerator and pull out a quarter bottle of Jack.

I mostly cleared out the apartment of liquor when I quit, but I saved this one bottle as a bail out.

I pull off the top and wave the bottle under my nose, the smell hitting me as I close my eyes.

If ever there was a time for a man to drink, it might be now.

I've got this whole plan. Get revenge on Toni. Use my worthless life to make theirs better.

Why did Kim have to get pregnant now?

But I don't bring the bottle to my lips.

Because I've got some fucking choices in front of me. If Kim is pregnant, there is no question in my mind whether or not the baby is mine.

I know who Kim is. And despite the fact that the sex is panty-melting hot, this is not a regular thing for her.

There hasn't been anyone else.

I shouldn't have accused her of seducing me at the wedding, it was all me. And I should have warned her, I detonate the lives of the people around me. It's what I do. It's why I'm better off going to jail.

That's what pushes me to bring the bottle to my nose again.

"What are you doing?"

I look up to see Kim in the hall wearing nothing but my discarded T-shirt.

Damn, she looks so good like that. Long legs, mussed hair.

"My mom was an alcoholic," I tell her. I set the bottle down on the counter. "I think I was too. I drank all the time, and it fueled my anger, my impulsivity. I got the worst of both my parents. All my siblings would tell you it's true."

She comes out of the hall and around the island. I don't even question pulling her into my arms, her soft scent wrapping around me as I fold her into my embrace.

"If you want me to assure you that you won't make your parents' mistakes, I'm probably the wrong person to ask. I just found out, I'm likely making my mom's biggest mistake of her life, so yeah..."

Right. All at once it hits me that Kim has the same hang-up I do. Fear of becoming her parent. It's why she's so sensitive about the topic of promiscuity. Probably why she was locked down so tight before she met me.

She'd never get pregnant on purpose, and I am an ass for even suggesting it, but we knew that already. I settle her closer, brushing a kiss on the top of her head. "We both have some choices to make."

"We do."

I slide a hand down her spine, closing my eyes. Mason is dad material. Hell, even Roman would make a good dad…but me?

I'm the guy who ruins everything. I'd ruin a kid. No question.

Still holding Kim, I reach for the cap and stuff it back on the bottle. I can't control what I did that night at Mason's wedding, the choices I made that impacted Kim, but I can control this.

I feel calmer just choosing to close the bottle. My arm around Kim, I kiss her forehead. "Want to go back to bed?"

"I could use a toothbrush," she says.

I dumped her bag right next to the elevator and so I leave her side to grab it now. Handing it to her, I run a hand through my hair. "Don't try to leave tonight, ok?"

She takes the bag, grimacing. "I don't…"

"Kim." I touch her cheek. "Your safest here, not out in Vegas in the middle of the night."

She gives a tentative nod and we both go back to the bedroom as she heads into the bathroom to brush her teeth. I sit on the edge of the bed and I'm not feeling so crazy anymore. Tonight, I'll be calm so Kim can be calm. She needs her sleep.

She comes back out and I peel back the covers for her to climb into the bed. She does and I immediately settle her into my side, pulling her close.

"Are you sure you want to snuggle tonight?" she asks, and I can feel her worry, the tension in her limbs.

"I'm sure."

She looks up at me but silence settles between us. I'm not sure what else to say. Instead, I stroke a hand down her back, but I can feel that she isn't relaxing into sleep.

Kissing her again, I swallow down a tightness in my throat. "I'm sorry for what I said."

She looks at me then, her eyes wide. "Leo."

"No. I shouldn't have said it. My temper is a bitch sometimes."

She settles her head on my chest her body relaxing. I lay there for a long time. I know I'm not sleeping much tonight, my brain is going a million miles a minute, but I want Kim to get some rest.

I hold still as she slips into sleep. As her breathing grows deep and even, I make some promises to do better.

My plans are going to have to change, even the ones involving the Carcettis. They have to go down, but I'm not sure I can go down with them. Maybe it's time I stop trying to be a vigilante and get some help from my family.

I finally drift off, my dreams full of my father, the choices he made, and how they've wreaked havoc on me and my brothers.

I've been so angry at him, and that anger has exploded out of me over all facets of my life.

But now…I could be the father. How am I going to do it differently? Not participate? Leave my kid so that I don't damage him? Or her…

I look at Kim as she sleeps on my chest. She bears scars too and they are from a man who never wanted to be a father.

She views herself as less, worthless. I hold her tighter. I'm no shrink but I can see how your father bailing on you might make you feel that way.

I shake my head. I don't even know if Kim is pregnant. It's too soon to think all this shit. Then again, I can't seem to not think it. My brain won't turn off.

What if she is pregnant? What man do I want to be?

Somehow, that thought calms me. Because I know I'm not going to be a selfish prick. I'm going to be a man who steps up.

The past few months have been about learning to do it right. I thought that meant falling on the sword, but maybe there is another way.

So yeah…

That is the thought that finally allows me to fall asleep.

My alarm goes off a few hours later and I jerk awake with the vague feeling that something is wrong.

Kim is already awake, staring at me with troubled eyes and everything comes crashing back. "I'm guessing morning sex is out?"

She actually smiles at that and then I give a small laugh too. Cause I'm pretty sure right now my job is to ease some of the tension.

"You get any sleep?" she asks, nipping at her lip.

"A little? You?"

"A bit." I kiss the top of her head before I pick up my phone. I fire off a text to Roman that I need his doctor and he instantly responds?

In house or in office?

In house means that it's off the books and discreet. A service we've had to use more than once.

In office. I message back. *Appointment for Kim.*

She injured?

I draw in a breath. I knew this question was coming. But I also know enough to know that Kim will need real medical care.

Missed her period.

Shit.

Yeah. There is nothing else to say. Not yet. And I'm not hiding or lying. I've done too much of that.

I get up from the bed, stretching. Kim's still laying down but she's staring up at me with these eyes like she's just waiting for something terrible to happen. So I lean in and kiss her, morning breath and all. "Let's take a shower."

"Together?"

"Fuck yeah." I know we're not having sex. "You think I'd miss an opportunity to touch you, princess?"

She nips at her lip. "Look. We both know I might be pregnant. You don't have to pretend that you still want me."

I know what her deal is, what makes her hurt, which is why I sit down and hold her face in mine. "Kim. Look down at my cock. I still want you."

I see her face flush at the same time she relaxes, her shoulders slumping. I know telling her that I still want to fuck her brains out isn't much, but apparently, it's enough.

My phone lights up, Roman sending another message. He's booked an appointment for nine in the morning with a partner group of doctors that does prenatal care.

They have on-site ultrasound machines.

Sometimes I wonder where Roman and Mason came from. Luke and I are knock-head kind of guys, we get that from our fathers.

Except lately, I see why being someone like Mason is an asset. I pull Kim from the bed, lacing our fingers together as we walk toward the bathroom.

I'm starting to come up with a plan but I'm going to wait, hold off and get all the information first, and then I'm going to act.

CHAPTER TWENTY

KIM

THE LAST HOUR has felt like a dream. Or maybe a nightmare.

I'm staring down a long strip of Ultrasound pictures, the little dot on the screen confirmation that I have made the one mistake I swore never to make.

I don't cry. I think I might be dried out.

Leo stayed by my side all through the exam, his fingers flexing in mine when the doctor played the heartbeat out loud with this little microphone attached to a machine. "Here that?" She'd smiled at us both. "That's the heartbeat of your baby! We can't always hear them at this stage so that means your baby's heart is really strong."

I tried to smile back but all I could feel was sick dread.

Then they'd taken us for an ultrasound where the tech had told us that everything looked really good.

I look at the pictures in my hand, reading the words.

KIMBERLY EVINGSTON

Approximate date of conception, July 14.

MASON AND CHARLOTTE'S WEDDING.

"You all right over there?" Leo asks, giving me a quick glance as he drives his car through Vegas traffic.

"I'm fine," I answer. Even I know I don't sound fine. "I'll be fine."

He gives the smallest nod. "Want to go back to my place?"

I shake my head. "No. I'll go back to mine. I should…" I'd been about to say pack. The plan was for me to stay with Leo until I moved to New York.

First, there is no point in going to New York if I'm pregnant. And while a few times today the idea of an abortion has popped in my head, I already know that I can't. What if my mom had gone that route?

But how I'll raise a child is a complete mystery to me. I don't even have enough money to pay for my class, I certainly don't have money for doctors. My head drops down a notch. I can return to Minneapolis now or I can try to finish out my degree. And at least for now, I still have my job at Temptation.

Could I make enough to put a down payment on a house? I don't even know how that works.

But maybe I could get a place and my mom could move in too. She could help me with the baby and…

She's going to be so disappointed with me.

My hands twist together.

"My place is probably more comfortable. You could take a bath. Sleep."

I shake my head. "I'm meeting Charlotte for lunch today."

"Ah." I see him hesitate out of the corner of my eye. "You going to tell her?"

I shake my head. "No. Not yet. I need to figure some stuff out. I…" My throat gets tight. There are the tears.

"We'll figure stuff out together," he says and then he places a hand over mine. "Promise."

I lift my head because his words feel so good. We've had sex like three times. This is not a marriage thing, I get that.

But if I could just do it a little better than my mom. Maybe have Leo be part of the baby's life so this kid doesn't feel like I did. I squeeze his hand, trying not to get ahead of myself.

He turns down Sunset Drive, nearing my apartment. As he pulls up to the curb in front of my place, he clears his throat. "I guess the first decision is whether or not to end the pregnancy."

He says the words carefully, but I still jump. "Is that what you want?" I don't know why I ask it like this. I already know how I feel.

"I'm asking you."

I draw in a breath to steady my nerves. "I don't think I could, to be honest."

He gives me a small smile, his thumb brushing over my cheek. "Ok. First decision made."

And then he opens his door, coming around the car to open mine. He helps me out, and once I'm standing, he pulls me close, bringing his mouth down on mine. It's a soft kiss. The kind that makes my breath catch as he holds my face. "Try to relax today. You didn't get much sleep."

He steps back, pulling a wallet out of his pocket. I blink down as he pulls out several bills. "And buy nice food, Kim. Stuff to make the spinach smoothies you like."

"I don't need—" It's a reflex. But he closes my hand over the bills.

"I know you won't spend what you made at Temptation, and you left your bag at my place anyway. I need to know, since you don't have access to my fridge, that you'll be eating plenty."

I shake my head. "Charlotte's taking me out. She'll—" But he kisses me again, silencing the words. And then he starts walking me to the door.

He doesn't come into the apartment, but when I walk in, Chandra and Kendall are both staring out the window watching Leo pull away.

They turn to me.

"Did he give you money?" Kendall asks.

"Of course, he did," Chandra answers, before she turns to me. "What did he give it to you for?"

"He's just paying me for sex," I answer, before I stomp off to my room. I thought coming here would give me space outside of Leo's world to think but Chandra sprints after me.

"That's bullshit. He was all possessive about where you were going to live yesterday."

I stop because she's right. Turning back to her, I cock my head to the side, as I ask, "If you were me, what would you think?"

"He's way into you," Kendall volunteers. "I mean the way he touched your face. That's like some Ryan Gosling shit right there," she says as she sighs. "How is he in bed?"

I blink at the juxtaposition, but I don't answer. The last thing I need to tell Kendall is that he makes my eyes roll back in my head on the regular. She'd stick to him like a fly to paper.

"Is he your boyfriend?" Chandra asks.

"I don't know," I shrug. "It's complicated."

"The best ones are," Chandra sighs as she leans her back against the wall. But then she stiffens again. "Hey. By the way…you know Melissa at the club?"

"Yeah," I shake my head because with Chandra conversations always just kind of bounce from topic to topic.

"She was talking about you last night before you came in and it was weird."

"Weird how?" My stomach twists as I remember Melissa telling me that Leo wanted to talk to me.

"She was on the phone, and she was telling someone what time you came in and that you were dating Mr. Kincaid."

My brows draw together. That is weird…

My head totally full, I go into my room and change into a dress and then head out for my lunch with Charlotte. I'm early but I could use some time to just meander.

I think about texting Leo and telling him about the Melissa thing but honestly, compared to everything else, it seems small. And I'm tired of sharing problems with Leo.

I think back to that guy on the plane who called me a hot mess. Maybe I am…my life is more of a mess than ever.

But I push those thoughts aside as I enter the restaurant.

It's a cute little French Bistro and Charlotte is glowing with happiness as she sits down, a few shopping bags in hand.

She pulls out a wrapped package from one. "For you."

I open the crisp white paper, finding a picture of myself inside a beautiful silver frame. I'm outside but I'm in a plié, the desert stretching out behind me. It's not the first picture Charlotte has taken of me, in fact she snaps them pretty often, but in this photo I'm different. I look really happy. Maybe that's not the right word. I look…serene. "When did you even take this?" Charlotte's pictures always have an emotional depth to them, but I don't know if I've ever seen myself like this. I'm always worried, always striving.

"It was out by the Las Vegas sign. I can't remember why we went. But I do remember that this little girl was trying to do a plié and you showed her how."

I blink at the picture remembering. It feels like a lifetime ago and yet I can still hear her laugh as she bent and lifted her little hand.

"Do you think you'll teach dance someday?"

"What?"

Charlotte gives me a smile. "I know you love to dance, but you always seem happiest when you're helping other people."

I look down at the picture. She isn't wrong. I loved teaching in my mom's studio in high school, not that it paid much. No one knows that better than my mom, that teaching dance is no way to make money. "Maybe."

"So…" Charlotte smiles, changing the subject. "Before I start gushing about married life, you have to tell me what is going on between you and Leo. Mason says that Leo is moving you into this new building."

"What?" I can feel my heartbeat accelerate. "When did Leo say that?"

"Yesterday." Charlotte's brow scrunches. "Are you all right?"

“I’m just my usual hot mess,” I whisper, taking a deep gulp of the water glass in front of me.

“You’re not a hot mess at all,” Charlotte shakes her head. “You’re one of the steadiest people I know."

"Really? Because I failed a class, didn’t graduate, I—"

Charlotte reaches for my hand. “Trying to reach for things, to stretch, means that sometimes you fall. You’re a dancer, you know that. It doesn’t make you a mess, it makes you strong and brave.”

My shoulders sink in relief. “Thanks, Charlotte. I needed to hear that.”

She wraps her hand about mine. “Is something going on?”

I told Leo I wouldn’t tell her but I’m not sure I can hold it in. Maybe I need her perspective. “Yes.”

“Has Leo hurt you? He can be a real loose cannon.”

“No, of course not. If anything, he’s more gentle and considerate than any guy…” And that makes me pause.

“Leo?” Charlotte asks, her brows drawn together in disbelief.

I think of him holding my hand this morning as the ultrasound tech pointed out the beating heart of the baby on the screen.

He has been nothing but helpful all while taking care of me. Part of why I shut down last night was because I just assumed his rejection was coming.

But he didn’t reject me at all. He apologized for his initial reaction, sat next to me that entire appointment, and then he offered to let me hang at his place.

I think I really need to talk to Leo and be honest about a few things and I’ll try not to let my fears get in the way of really listening to what he has to say.

I think for the first time in a long time, I actually have a bit of real hope.

CHAPTER TWENTY-ONE

KIM

THE REST of the day is quiet, I even nap for a few hours before I head into work. There are no rehearsals on Saturdays, so I don't go in until after six.

Leo isn't there yet, I think he's taking care of stuff at other clubs. At least I'm hoping because I half expected him to offer me a ride and he didn't…

Which I don't mind. I like walking. Clears the head. And I'm still an independent woman, but changes in his behavior make me nervous and that little bit of hope I'd been feeling deflates like a popped balloon.

But I paste on a smile and head into the club, quietly slipping into the locker room.

"Hey," Samantha calls with a friendly wave.

"Hey." I smile as I turn to her, glad for a friendly face.

"Do you have a couple minutes to show me a few moves?"

My smile grows. "Of course." Teaching is just what I need to push away my worries. We head to a quiet back room where I spend some time helping her with a few new moves and some smoother transitions, which dancers frequently overlook, but when it comes to tips, I'm convinced they help keep the audience's attention.

It's a great way to warm up and as much as I helped Samantha, I feel better too. More grounded.

I return to my locker and change from my warm-up leotard into my leather uniform. Slipping into my three-inch heels, I sit at my vanity to paint on my make up. Just like any performance, it's not normal everyday makeup, but bold dark slashes of color to add drama.

I'm adding exaggerated wings about my eyes and a striking lipstick. My hair is in my usual straight ponytail that I only wear when I dance.

I have no idea how long I'll be able to stay thin enough to perform, but I feel the pressure to make money while I can. I'm going to crush it tonight.

I should know better than to think I'm on top of life. The moment I do, something always goes wrong…

The door to the locker room bursts open, a furious-looking Leo stands in the doorway.

Women change out in the open in here. I've never seen him enter unless it's really early or really late hours, so I sit up, blinking in surprise.

He fills the entire doorway, his huge frame looking even larger than normal. I swear, he grows bigger when he's angry.

And he is. I have no idea what's the matter but it's something. The energy rolls off him in pulsing waves.

He pauses for what is probably only a second, but the air is sucked out of the room, silence falling.

"Mr. Kincaid," Melissa says into the silence. I look back at her, but she doesn't look at me or Leo. She's texting on her phone instead.

The flash of a large diamond catches the light. Did she always have that?

But I can't focus on her because Leo is stalking toward me, his brow slashed into an angry line, his jaw hard enough to cut granite.

I set down my lipstick, turning toward him in my chair.

I know most people would be scared out of their gourd by an angry Leo, but it's never a feeling I have around him.

Whatever happens between us, Leo would never hurt me. And the last few weeks he's been the break wall that's held back the storms.

"What. The. Fuck," he says, stopping just in front of me so that I have to notch my chin up. "Are you doing here?"

My mouth opens and then closes as I stare him, my eyes narrowing into slits. I might have my insecurities, but I am not down for public intimidation. "I work here."

I didn't think it was possible, but he draws up even taller. "I'm taking you home right now."

"What? No." I don't get up. "Why?"

"Because," he grits out through his teeth. He doesn't step back which means he's crowding my space. I don't like it one bit. "You're pr—"

I stand. I weigh half of what Leo does, but I'm an expert at how to use my body and I use that knowledge now, setting my shoulder in his stomach that sends him back three steps as he doubles over. "Leo." Every dancer is hearing me use his first name. "Not here."

He stands up but keeps his distance, his eyes still fierce. "I don't want you here."

"Are you firing me?" I cross my arms over my chest. I can't stop him if that's his choice, but I won't forgive him either. There is no reason for it.

"You know I'm not."

My chin notches and I stare for a second before I calmly return to my seat to finish my makeup.

I grab my lipstick and start to reapply it, aware that every eye in the place is on us. Leo waits for another second before he closes the distance between us once again and snatches the lipstick from my hand.

I gasp, trying to stand again, but this time he's ready for me and sidesteps my shoulder, wrapping an arm about me to lift me off the ground.

I'm completely outraged and enraged in this moment. Did he just pick me up and humiliate me in front of everyone?

Even Charlotte warned me about Leo's temper, and I'm seeing it now.

But picking me up has my legs swinging and I let the momentum swing them even higher. And when they are as high as they can go, I send them arcing back down, my muscles behind them as the toe of my pointed heel crashes into Leo's shin.

"Fuck, Kim!" Leo roars right before he drops me. I just catch myself, straightening with my finger in his face.

"Try that again." I might be having a shit run of luck, and I may worry that I'm not good enough, but nobody physically intimidates me. That brings out the fight in me. And the thing about Leo is that in the bedroom, he's always put me on some pedestal that has allowed me to relax enough to really enjoy myself. "And you're going to meet my temper."

I'm not enjoying this at all. I brush past him, starting for the door.

I can hear the crowds filing into the club, the music firing up and I know the cages will rise soon.

If Leo wants to suggest another method by which I'll support our child, I'm all ears. But I'm not going to be manhandled into doing what he wants.

And I'm not leaving my best chance at making money because…I don't even know what his problem is.

I open the locker room door, starting down the back hall by the bathrooms and then the office, making my way to the back stairs.

A hand grabs my arm and I partially turn, spinning my arm to break the grip. I guess Leo's not done and now that we have a bit of privacy, I'm ready for another round. But as I turn, I see a man that's not Leo behind me.

It's a man I distantly recognize as the one who was in the hall right before Bobby showed up. Slick hair, slimy grin, toothpick…

I only have one second to process before he raises a gun pointing it right in my face. "We meet again, Kim."

A scream builds in my throat.

CHAPTER TWENTY-TWO

LEO

IT TAKES me two seconds to recover, spinning to follow Kim out of the locker room.

I can feel all the dancers' eyes on me, but I don't look at anyone else. I know what I just did, and regret is already tugging at my chest. When I realized Kim had come to work, I lost my temper.

I've been way better, but I'm a man who is working on change and that means sometimes I fail. But I think I fucked this one up good.

As I go to follow Kim down the hall, Melissa steps in front of me. "Hey, boss."

I look down at her, wondering why she'd be blocking me now. I'm clearly going after Kim. What would be important enough to interrupt? "I'll get back to you." I start to go around her, but she reaches out, grabbing my arm to stop me.

I like Melissa. She's a good employee, and easy to work with. She's pretty too, in a way that's not my type, but I can see the appeal. Customers like her.

Still, we've never had the kind of relationship where we touched each other for any reason and it's downright strange she's doing it now.

Which is when I catch the ring on her finger. I pay Melissa well but not five-carat-diamond well. "When did you get that?"

She doesn't grin or look happy. In fact, she winces. And that's when I know something shady is going down.

I push past her and out into the hall and start toward the back. If Kim went anywhere, she went up to the platform, but my heart is racing in my chest.

Something isn't right and I don't just mean how I just fucked up in the locker room. And I know I did. I lost it when I saw her all decked out in leather.

She's the mother of my child, she shouldn't be swinging around in a cage. I know I sound like a complete asshole, but I've got more money than I know what to do with. I just need the chance to tell Kim that she has all the choices in the world.

Because the entire time I was away from her today, all I could think about was holding her in my arms and taking care of her and our baby.

I draw in a shaky breath as I round the corner and then stop cold...

Kim is standing in the center of the hall with a gun to her head. Little Anthony Carcetti, nephew to the Italian Mafia boss behind her, one hand on her throat, the other on the gun.

My chest nearly explodes as I stop. "What the—"

Anthony gives me that slimy smile of his. "Leonard." And then he presses the gun against Kim's temple. I hear her whimper. "My uncle sends his regards."

"You are shitting—"

"You're not the only one who's been spying," he snarks, the smile disappearing. "But I bet you didn't even notice I've been watching. Your mistake."

My hands come up, my fingers splaying out. "Since when do we involve women in our business?"

Beyond the quiet of the hall, I can hear the club, already full. At any moment, someone could walk this way. A dancer or a club member just looking to use the restroom could end up right in the middle of this. I take a step forward, not looking at Kim or the fear shining in her eyes.

I need to focus. There is no way my shit is going to hurt Kim.

"We included her when you tipped a slot machine and then turned in footage of my cousin to the police."

My lip curls. "If we're counting sins, you've got a few to your name too. For example, can we discuss how this isn't the first time you've pulled a gun here." I take another step.

"You put our top guy in prison," Little Anthony snarks back.

"That doesn't mean I hurt one of your women. You're out of bounds."

He presses the gun tighter to Kim's temple. Her eyes squeeze shut, and my legs shake. I wouldn't be this scared if the gun were at my head, but something about her being in danger has me frantic on the inside.

It's a dirty move involving Kim and an unwritten rule that we don't. I will kill Anthony for this. I've got the most gangster in me, we all know it. He picked the wrong Kincaid to fuck with.

His hand slides from Kim's neck and over her chest, resting just above her leather-clad tits.

My fingers flex as he presses his lips to the shell of her ear. "You're a hot one, aren't you?"

I cannot afford to lose my cool. Drawing in a deep breath, I inch a little closer. What would Mason do?

He'd think. He'd put the pieces together. He'd come up with a...

Little Anthony brushes his fingers down over her right tit and I let out a rumbling growl as the details click together. "How is Melissa going to feel about you touching her like that?"

He snaps his attention back to me. "None of your fucking business."

I've found one weakness. Is that an engagement ring on her finger? Looked like it. Is he working her to get to me or does he care about her? "She is a hot number. Nice curves."

Some of the fear leaves Kim's eyes, replaced with what I think might be irritation. Good. It'll help her.

My temper has long been a problem. More so, because I act without thinking. That, and I can be a real selfish prick sometimes.

But I see the blood start to rise in Anthony and I know I've hit the wound that I need to force him into emotional decisions. "She tell you I fucked her a couple times?"

Kim is going to hate me. I know it.

I steal a quick glance at her, and I nearly wilt in relief. She doesn't look pissed, in fact, she gives me a near imperceptible nod of approval. She gets it.

"Shut the fuck up, you did not."

The gun lowers a fraction of an inch and I move closer. "Oh, I did. It was average. Forgettable. At least for me. I know you've heard that I've got some large equipment..."

I'm being my most dickish self. But he's threatening my woman, and I don't fucking like it.

"Fuck you," he spits out. "You're going to pay for that." And then he reaches back up and gives Kim's tit a good fucking squeeze.

I hear a woman cry, but it's not Kim.

Melissa rushes toward me, passing me by, her face is full of hurt and rage as she makes a rush at Anthony.

I grab her by the hair, yanking her back and wrapping a hand around her neck. I'm not hurting her, but I could.

Anthony points the gun at me instead of Kim and I unwind. I'd much rather take the bullet than watch her get shot.

"Why don't you tell him, Melissa? Tell him how you screamed my name and begged me to fuck you harder. Make you cum."

"I didn't!" she cries. "It's not true."

Anthony is bright red, a vein popping out of his temple as he shoves Kim to the side and charges toward me.

But she's way smarter and far more athletic than him and she swings around, hooking him behind the knee with her ankle. It sends him crashing forward as his hands fly in the air and the gun goes off.

It echoes down the hall, the screams of the crowd filling the place, but I'm not worrying about that. The bullet whizzes above my head, entering the ceiling.

I toss Melissa to the side and hurl myself at Anthony. He hits the ground hard, his hands splaying out in front of him to catch his weight. Stopping short, I give his hand with the gun a hard fucking stomp. I hear the bones crack and break.

Satisfaction courses through me. Bending down, I yank the gun from his hand, pointing it at his head.

I've still got my boot on his hand. "In my office," I bark at Kim. "Lock it."

She does as I say without question.

Melissa is leaning against the wall, her face pale, but I'm not dealing with her yet. "I lean down close to Anthony, putting more pressure on his hand as he cries out. "The last time you fired a shot in this club, the police weren't called. We didn't quite have the sway then that we have now."

I know what I'm going to do. I'd just resigned myself to not going to prison but in this moment...it's the best way to pick off a major player in the Carcetti operation.

"Fuck you," Anthony spits out a cry. "For what?"

"You can't go around firing guns in clubs, you asshole." But we've got video footage of him murdering a man here two years ago and that, along with what he just tried to do to Kim, should be enough history to put Little Anthony Carcetti away for a long time.

The only problem? I've been withholding evidence. And that's going to blow back on me. It sends a sharp pain shooting down my chest. That has always been the plan, for me to take the fall. But now... things are different.

Melissa starts to slide away, I catch her out of the corner of my eye, and I point a finger at her. "Don't you fucking move."

"Mr. Kincaid," she says on a sob. "I didn't think—"

"You'll never work in this town again," I grit out. "You won't even be hired as a cocktail waitress. You can marry him, but he is going to be in prison for the rest of his life."

"Fuck you—"

I press harder on his broken hand, and he cries out as the sound of sirens fill the air.

"You don't think we got rid of the evidence two years ago, do you? What debt did you think Mason was calling in?" I grab Anthony by the hair, lifting his head. "Yes, you owe us money. But that's not the real danger we pose to you, is it? Did you think that you could threaten Kim and make that evidence disappear? You fucked up."

I curl my lip, dropping his head again. I was going to kill him but as I lift my boot, I can see his hand is a mangled mess. He's never firing a gun again. It's enough. I'm a new man after all.

The club has cleared out. Temptation will need some time to recover, but we'll do what we did last time Anthony Carcetti shot it up, and do a big reopen.

Honestly, Temptation is the least of my concerns. For all I know, I won't even be here to see it. Kim is going to hate me for taking the fall, for leaving her now. But I'll try to make her understand. This is the best way to keep her and the baby safe. The Carcetti scum needs to be taken off the streets.

It's going to be a long night, but at least Kim is safe. And once I get her tucked in my bed, we need to have a real talk about the future.

She might not want me after all this, but I whatever she chooses, I will provide for her and for the baby.

If I'd had any doubts, Anthony Carcetti made my job crystal clear. I never thought I'd say this, but I might actually have to thank him for that.

Nah.

But it's time Kim understands what I see for our future.

CHAPTER TWENTY-THREE

KIM

THE REST of the evening passes like a nightmare.

The police arrive first, and Carcetti isn't the only one in cuffs.

I watch a cop push Leo against the wall, slapping metal on his wrists. "You Kincaids have been stirring trouble lately," some middle-aged balding cop sneers in Leo's ear.

Carcetti is taken out by ambulance and Melissa has disappeared. I give a statement, but I'm not convinced the cop is listening to a word I'm saying, his eyes all over me.

It's then that Mason enters the club. I've got to hand it to him. He sucks all the air out of the room. Well, him and the team of lawyers behind him.

One stations himself at my side, another at Leo's, who is out of cuffs in a matter of seconds.

Everything gets a lot friendlier when the video tapes are played back, Carcetti grabbing me, holding a gun to my head.

Even Leo stomping his hand is clearly self-defense.

I watch as Leo whispers in Mason's ear and Mason gives the smallest smile with a nod of agreement.

Leo disappears and then comes out again, holding a small computer drive in his hand, that he hands to the lead investigator.

I have no idea what he's giving the man, but he crosses back to Mason. I start moving toward them too. Any anger that I had toward Leo has been completely replaced by a deep need to curl against him. I want to be in his arms. I'm a few feet from his side when I hear him say, "If it blows back, I'll take the heat, but we've got a few things to discuss first."

Mason catches my gaze, not answering as he looks from me to Leo.

But Leo doesn't say anything to his brother. Instead, he turns to me too, opening his arms.

I step into his embrace without a moment's hesitation, letting him wrap me up.

My head comes to his chest, as I hold onto his waist. "Do we get to leave soon?"

"Yeah, baby, we do. Tired?"

I nod. "Yeah, I'm tired and I want to go home."

He grazes a kiss across my forehead. "I'll wrap up as soon as I can, but I can have someone take you home now if you can't wait. Roman or Jake can drive you."

I honestly don't know if he means my place or his and I'm not taking the chance I get dropped off at my apartment.

Chandra will be murder. She's been blowing up my phone with questions as it is.

And I need to speak with Leo. Just be next to him without all this noise. I just want to stretch out against him, feel his strength next to me.

Tonight was so crazy and when his arms are around me, I feel like I can breathe again.

"I had the bed sent..." Mason says. I'm trying to figure that one out when he adds, "And Roman packed all the essentials himself and brought them over."

My brow scrunches, confusion making me look between the brothers, as Leo says, "Thanks for taking care of those details."

Mason waves his hand. "You've been a little busy tonight. And in case I don't say it later, nice job taking down another Carcetti. Big Toni is going to be pissed and that's a problem we're going to have to handle soon."

"Vendetti's younger brother has been quiet too, but he won't stay quiet. That's a coiled snake waiting to strike."

"You're right," Mason eyes Leo, appreciation shining in his eyes. "You've got some plans?"

"Toni, yes. I think I've got something figured out. It's a good one too. The younger Vendetti, I'm still working on it."

Mason slaps Leo on the back. I'm still in Leo's arms so the smack reverberates through both of us. "Keep thinking. I look forward to hearing your plans."

Leo nods. "Can we talk tomorrow? There are a few other details we need to discuss."

Mason nods. "I'll come to your place with brunch."

It takes another half hour but we finally leave. I slide into the seat of Leo's car, closing my eyes. "You're not bringing me to my apartment, are you?"

"Fuck no," Leo answers as he climbs in. "In fact, you might as well pack your stuff tomorrow. There is no way you're sleeping without being next to me."

"Giving orders again?" But I smile, relaxing into the seat. I have no desire to be more than two feet from Leo for a while.

"Baby," he says, and I can hear the softening of his voice. "Please. I'll go crazy if—"

I turn to him, opening my eyes. "I was teasing. Maybe poor timing, but I promise, I'm as eager to stay next to you as you are to have me there."

He reaches for my hand then, pulling the back of my fingers against his lips to give them a long kiss.

I sigh out my pleasure at the feel of his skin on mine. "Does Mason know that after you bluster, you're a big softie?"

Leo looks over at me, cocking a brow. "No one gets soft Leo but you, baby. Don' t you know that?"

I did not know that. My belly flutters as I clear my throat. "Are we talking about the baby tonight?"

He shakes his head. "I don't know. It feels like..."

"There's a lot going on?"

"Yeah."

Leo turns onto the highway, and I realize we're leaving Las Vegas proper. I lift my head. "Where are we going?"

"The Carcettis live in Summerlin," he says as though that answers my question. "So naturally, we are going to Southern Highlands."

"What's in Southern Highlands?"

"Your house."

"My house?" I sit up, straighter. "What does that even mean?"

"Well, technically, it's our house. Or, more accurately, a Kincaid house. Mason picked it up on a short sale. Even the rich go bankrupt."

"How much real estate does Kincaid Enterprises own?"

He winks at me. "I told Mason this morning I wanted to take you out of the city. The plan is moving bit sooner than I imagined, and I had every intention of asking you first—"

"Questionable."

He smiles. "But tonight, I think we'll both sleep better in a place no one is going to look."

"Why would you call it my house then?"

"I thought you could raise the baby there."

My head is spinning. Is he giving me a house? "I really appreciate the thought, but I don't have the kind of money that would allow me to even keep the lights on in a house in Southern Highlands."

He shakes his head. "In case it wasn't clear, I have no intention of leaving you to raise this baby on your own. And what babies need most, besides love, is money."

My breath catches. We're pulling off the highway and it takes everything in me not to climb over the console and into his lap while he drives.

It only takes a few minutes before we're pulling into a gated community and then into a driveway for a house that is circled by a large high wall and thick metal gates.

There is a guard at the gate and a few more out on the lawn. "Who are they?"

"Kincaid Enterprises security men we keep on retainer. We are not taking any chances."

I swallow down a lump. The car comes to a stop and I do exactly what I wanted a minute ago. I'm over the console, my ass landing in Leo's lap, my feet still in my seat. I wedge myself between Leo and the steering wheel. There is barely room, but I don't care as my lips crash against his, my hands threading into his hair.

CHAPTER TWENTY-FOUR

LEO

KIM'S ASS grinds into my cock and I'm raging hard in a second.

I have no idea how I'm getting us out of this car with any grace, not that I care what the guards think, but I cannot have Kim take a tumble.

I'm glad Temptation is closing temporarily. She would have been murder to keep out of the club. She's got it in her head that she needs to make money, but that's just ridiculous.

Whatever dancing she does from here on out will be for the beauty, joy, fame…whatever.

She won't need to make money. But that's going to take some adjusting, at least for Kim.

And I appreciate that. But the house, the allowance, I'm going to need her to take it. Turning over an old tape to the police has the potential to create some real problems.

There will be questions about why I haven't given it to the police sooner. As the head of the club division at Kincaid Enterprises, that's my pile of shit to own, even if Mason was the man who made the decision to not strike against the Italians two years ago when Anthony Carcetti killed a low man within the ranks of the Russian Bratva behind Temptation doors.

In the past I would have been angry at Mason for pushing the pile of shit onto me. But the truth is, Mason has made us strong. And he made the right decision then. I know it deep in my gut.

Which is why, if someone has to take the fall, I'll take it, knowing that Mason will keep Kim wrapped in a protective bubble until I'm back. I hate to leave her, but this is a move I've been preparing for. Not that I want to think about it anymore tonight.

Right now, all I want to do is bury myself deep inside her.

My tongue is in her mouth, tangling with hers and my hands are everywhere. I'm actually starting to hate the leather suit because I can feel all her curves, but I can't get my hands on her skin.

I pop open my door, not breaking the kiss and slide one foot out of the car. But I'm not going to be able to lift her out. There just isn't enough room.

She finally pulls back from the kiss and reaching up, she grabs the frame of the car, lifting herself off my lap and curling her legs so that she can swing them past me before they land on the ground as she stands outside the car.

"Coming?" she asks innocently.

"What the fuck? How did you do that?"

She shrugs. "I'm a professional dancer."

I step from the car standing next to her and I see her smile falter. "Or I was."

My hand comes to her hip, pulling our bodies tight together. "I'll get you to New York, baby, promise."

She cocks her head to the side, giving me a long look. "Do you really mean that?"

We haven't really talked about the baby, or the future, or even the past. But I'm going to make this right. "I do."

Behind me, a throat clears. I turn to the guard, a man I recognize, as he gives me a nod. "Perimeter is secured. No sign of anything or anyone."

I nod back. "Keep me posted if there is any trouble."

He is doing an excellent job of not looking at Kim, but I see his gaze dart over to her, his chin drawing back as his chest puffs out.

His eyes slide down her and I make a note to inform Mason that he's going to have to hire different security if I'm not around. This guy has taken note. We're going to have to hire uglier guards if I'm not here.

Hand on her hip in a possessive hold, I walk Kim inside.

There is no furniture in most of the rooms, but I've been in the house one other time, so I lead her up the stairs and into the master.

The room is huge, the bed massive and, in the closet are my clothes and shoes. "Roman did all this?"

"He's like Mason, organized, methodical, deliberate. They can both move mountains when they want. And the fuckers do it with efficiency."

She looks back at me, a small smile on her face. "And you don't?"

I live in the grey more than either of my other brothers. Which is why everyone will believe that I was the one who held those tapes back.

And I'll be the one who actually gets the revenge my family is seeking because…I'm willing to do the things Mason and Roman are not.

It suddenly occurs to me that I don't have their planning abilities, but my instincts have led me to exactly where we need to be to get what we want.

Is that what Kim is saying with that smile?

She's still in her dancing costume and I move to her side, pulling her up against my body. "What do you say we get you out of that and into a shower?"

"You think this one has one of those sprayers?" she asks with a giggle.

Grabbing her by the ass, I pull her tight into my hips, my cock pressing into her soft belly. "We're about to find out."

And then I wrap my other hand around her, lifting her to carry her into the bathroom.

Not that I need to hold her at all. Her legs wrap around me and the strength of them could hold her up without my support at all.

But there is also no way I'm taking my hands from her ass. In fact, I use my grip to grind our pelvises together, pulling a low needy moan from her throat.

I swallow that down, even as I use one of my hands to tug at the hidden zipper in the back of the leather suit.

Today, I might rip this thing to shreds to get it off her.

The zipper sticks halfway down and so I give it hard yank, hearing it pull away from the leather as the stitching gives.

She pulls back, her brows lifting. "Is that coming out of my pay?"

I kiss her again, my tongue thrusting into her mouth as I step into the bathroom. I already know I'm going to fuck her hard against the shower wall and my balls are tingling with the need to be inside her.

"I'll buy you ten of these if you let me rip them off you."

"Are you going to make a belly cut out?" she asks but I see the wince.

What the fuck does that mean? "Belly cut out?"

"What if…" She looks away then. "What if I'm horrid-looking when I'm really pregnant? What if I never recover? What if…"

"Hey," I let her hold herself with her legs that are still wrapped around my waist. "If you think you're going to get out of being jack-hammered because of a little baby jiggle, you are sorely mistaken."

She laughs. "Jackhammered? Sore might be the operative word there."

My kiss is slower and softer as I hold her face between my hands. "My point is that I'm not going anywhere."

She shakes her head. "You really mean that? You're going to stick with me?"

"I'm sticking."

She kisses me again, and it's like she's trying to suck the cum from my balls up my throat. I don't mind. In fact, I fucking love it.

I know that Kim is worried that I'll split. But at some point, she may regret being so deep in with me.

That's too bad, because I'm not letting her go ever.

I finally set her down, yanking the suit off her until she's in nothing but her thong. I get in the shower and turn it on, not caring that I'm still dressed.

The spray hits me even as I yank my clothes off, tossing them out of the shower, and then I tug her in.

She's still wearing the underwear, but I actually think it's going to feel even better as I take down the removable head and set it to full blast.

And then I settle her back to my chest, sliding a knee between her legs to spread her open.

Her leg wraps around mine.

Kim is so athletic, it makes sex extra fucking fantastic and I take full advantage, wrapping one of her arms around my head to open her body even wider.

Sliding my hand down her front, I stop to tweak one of her nipples as I point the shower head right at her clit.

She jolts against me, her head tossing back. "Oh God, Leo!" she says in a keening cry.

I nip at her neck, tweaking her nipple harder.

It takes all of ten seconds for the first orgasm to rocket through her, which is fine by me. I'm not fucking around tonight.

I need to be inside her, which is why I spin her around and yank down her thong, tossing it to the corner of the shower. Then, I lift her up again. Her legs naturally circle my waist as I take two handfuls of her fantastic fucking ass and then I slam into her already drenched pussy.

"You're so wet for me baby," I grunt as I lift her up and pump into her again.

Normally, I'd expect a bit of snark from her sassy mouth but instead, she arches, tossing her head back and pulling my cock deeper into her body.

I'm almost feral as I pump into her. Something has shifted.

This is my woman. Now. Later.

I think I might be in love.

I squeeze my eyes shut, trying to process that as I slow the pace a bit.

She's arched in a way that exposes the smooth, long column of her neck, her tits bouncing with my every thrust.

I'm in love with Kim. And I will do anything, and I mean anything, to protect our baby. Toni Carcetti, he's going down. Jail? Murder? I don't fucking care.

I dig my fingers deeper into her ass, wanting more of her of her body touching mine. More of my cock inside her.

She's making these keening cries and whimpers, her pussy like a vice around my cock.

I know she's getting close, and I ease back to tease her, and to enjoy the moment.

Her chin snaps forward, her eyes meeting mine with an accusation that might make a lesser man wither.

"You want to come, baby?"

"Yes," she moans, her body arching again, the invitation completely clear. "Make me cum, Leo."

"I'm gonna make you cum, baby, don't you worry. You're going to cum so hard, I'm going to get you pregnant twice."

Her mouth drops open as she stares at me. But I don't give her a chance to argue because I ratchet up the pace again, pistoning in and out of her while her legs clamp around my waist like a vise.

"Please, Leo," she sobs, clenching and unclenching her thighs to pull me deeper in and release me further out. "God. Yes. Fuck. Yes."

She's so tight around me now, her grip is almost painful, which only makes it better as I swell, my balls so tight, they are about to explode.

Finally, she breaks, her scream echoing off the bathroom walls. It's the final straw for me, and a second later, I'm pumping her full of cum. "Kim," I roar in her ear. "Baby. Take it all."

She's still mewling in my ear, little sounds that are maybe supposed to be words, I'm not sure.

I take one hand off her ass and brace it against the wall because I swear, that wrung out every molecule of energy I have.

I've never had an orgasm like that. I swear, I could get knocked over with a feather right this second.

"We fuck great in a bed," I say, my head falling forward into her neck. "But, my God, woman, we fuck amazing outside it."

She gives a little gasping laugh, like she's still struggling for air and some satisfied part of me loves that I've managed to render her speechless.

Finally, she lifts her head to meet my gaze. "Let's go to bed," she says, her muscles softening against my body.

"Tired, baby?" I kiss along her collarbone, gaining enough strength to stand up so that I can turn off the shower and carry us both back out to the bedroom.

"Yeah," she says with a sigh. "I feel like I could sleep for a week."

"Mason's coming for late breakfast tomorrow, but you'll be able to sleep as late as you want, all right?"

"All right," she sighs as I lay her down in the massive bed and slide in behind her.

Pulling her back tight into my chest, I wrap her in my arms, my knee settling between her thighs.

"Leo?"

"Yeah, baby?"

"I'm glad you're going to be part of the baby's life."

"Me too," I say as I slide a hand down to her stomach and spread out my fingers. "I'm the only Kincaid who has reproduced. I think this officially means I'm more potent than either of my brothers."

She snorts then. "Or worse at using birth control."

There's my snarky girl. I nuzzle into her neck. "I might make a shit father. Mine sucked."

"Mine too," she answers. "I think showing up is the first bar to be being decent, though."

"I think decent is a realistic goal." I'm not sure I'll meet it, though. I do know one thing. No one will hurt Kim or my child. I'll see to that.

CHAPTER TWENTY-FIVE

KIM

SLEEPING LATE, I wake up to the sound of the blender. A smile tugs at my lips as I stretch, my body sore.

Sex with Leo is equivalent to hours of dancing in terms of stiff muscles.

I hear him coming up the stairs and I pick my head up to look around the massive bedroom I am in. Its space is made even bigger by the muted creams it's been decorated with. Thick carpet covers the floor and gauzy linen curtains adorn the windows.

He called this place mine, but I know he isn't giving me a house.

Still, it's nice to think that he plans to be part of the baby's life and that he's willing to help. And for now, I'm going to take this opportunity to figure some things out.

First on the list, finishing my degree.

Working at Temptation isn't going to be an option after last night, which means I need money for school.

I hate asking men for things. It feels like I'm just setting myself up for disappointment when I do, but as Leo enters the room wearing nothing but a pair of athletic pants, I sit up, stretching.

He stops in the door, his eyes scanning down my naked torso.

I grin because, despite the amazing view of this shirtless man, he's made two spinach smoothies, one smaller, and one very large. "For me?" I ask, stretching my arms over my head as my stomach grumbles. I'm so hungry and a smoothie sounds amazing.

"For you," he answers, moving deeper into the room. "After you're done, I've got something else for you."

"What's that?"

He glances down to his groin and my eyes follow, noting the very large erection already tenting his pants. I laugh as he reaches the bed and I extend my hand for the smoothie.

He pulls it back, not letting me take it as he leans over and captures my mouth in a fierce but brief kiss.

Then he pulls away and hands me my smoothie.

I take it, drinking several long swallows. I hate asking for things, but I can't just think about me.

I want Leo's promise about sticking around to be true. But if I take this favor now, I'll be better able to take care of the baby, no matter what happens. And that has me drawing in a fortifying breath as I lower my smoothie.

"Leo?"

He takes his first sip of his smoothie before he lowers his glass too, his brow furrowing. "You sound very serious."

"I..." I lick my lips, drawing in a deep breath. "I need to ask a favor."

"Hell has frozen over."

I smile, my chin dipping. "You're not wrong. But..." I draw in a deep breath as his hand skims down my ribs to settle into the curve of my waist. "I'd really like to finish my degree and I'm short on cash—"

"Done."

I blink back my surprise. "Done?"

"How much?" He crosses to a small desk in the corner and opens a drawer, pulling out his checkbook.

"How did you know your checkbook would be in there?" I ask, rising from the bed.

"I told you, Roman is ridiculously good with the details." He takes out a pen, pulling the cap off with his teeth and then starts writing.

"Well, I have two thousand from that first night, so I'd need three more to pay for the class."

Leo looks back at me with narrowed eyes. "Kim."

"What?"

He shakes his head. "I'll write the check for twenty."

"Twenty dollars?"

"Twenty thousand."

I nearly choke on my next swallow of smoothie. "Leo, I couldn't possibly—"

"You can and you will. Think of it as fun money. You see a crib you want to buy, you buy it. Maternity clothes. Get your nails done. I don't care."

"Leo. You're not my—"

"If you say I'm not your boyfriend, I don't care if you're pregnant, I will put you over my knee."

I get instantly wet, like soaking wet as I stop in front of him. I'm tempted to say it just so he does it. "You'd spank me, daddy?"

I don't know why I call him this. It just pops out.

But he tosses the checkbook to the side, grabbing me by the ass and pulling me roughly against him.

With fumbling hands, I set my smoothie on the desk, my appetite for food forgotten.

I love having my legs wrapped around his waist. I don't know why but it's both a place of power and vulnerability. I'm totally open to him and yet also wrapped around him and I don't hesitate as I wrap my arms and legs around his torso, coming off the ground, pressing my pussy to his cock in the best way.

His hand lifts from my ass, only to smack against the soft flesh... hard. I feel the sting, pleasure rocketing through me as I arch to grind against his cock still covered by his athletic pants.

His hand smacks my ass several more times, the pain only

increasing the pleasure. The thing about being an athlete, which dancers are, is that gratification always comes with pain and my pleasure is only amplified by the sting.

Grabbing my stinging red ass cheek with one hand, his palm presses flat against me, his fingers dig into my flesh, he uses his other hand to yank down his pants.

They don't even make it to his thighs before he's thrusting inside me, his hard length filling me so full that I scream out my pleasure.

He spins us, and bending us both, my back lands flat on the desk as he thrusts into me again causing the entire desk to shake.

I know the desk is well made, everything in this house is, and I might wonder if the force he's fucking me with should cause the piece to rattle like that, but I'm too busy being thoroughly and roughly ravaged as he grabs my hips and sets a pace that turns my body molten.

I cry out at the pleasure over and over, the desk biting into my back in the best way.

I know I'm getting loud, I can't help it, Leo does that to me. My orgasm is building as I scratch at his forearms, keeping him as tight to my body as I can.

I'm going to cum, I can feel it building as I squeeze my eyes shut, my entire body so taut, I feel like I might break.

Stars appear behind my lids and I finally orgasm, screaming out as I cum.

Leo roars out an orgasm of his own, pumping into me over and over as I feel him filling me.

I can barely move as he collapses on top of me.

"I'd better check with the doctor," he murmurs into my collarbone.

"About?"

"Fucking you like that..." His hands are sliding up and down my body, the lion turned cub now that he's emptied inside of me.

I shake my head. "I seriously doubt that sex, even sex like that, hurts a group of cells the size of a pin head."

But I appreciate his worry. He wraps his arms under me and lifts me. I groan softly, all the pain plus some new aches making me creak as I move.

Leo winces. "We'll have to take a break from hard sex on hard surfaces," he murmurs into my ear.

"I'll be fine. I'm used to recovery time after a hard workout."

"How about a hot bath to soothe some of those aches?"

I smile against his cheek as he carries me into the bathroom. He starts the tub and gently sets me down when a hard knock sounds on our bedroom door.

His face goes hard, as he takes my hand and helps me into the bath. "I'll be right back, baby."

Baby… And he wonders why I called him daddy.

He closes the bathroom door as I sink into the water, but I don't relax. Who is it? Is something wrong?

Leo appears again, athletic pants back on. "Mason is here. I'm going to talk to him while you finish your bath, baby. Take your time."

And then he disappears again.

But I start washing myself in earnest. As much as I'd like a long soak, the brothers are going to be talking about what happened last night and what to do next. And I'd like to hear some of what they have to say.

CHAPTER TWENTY-SIX

Leo

I walk back through the bedroom, not bothering with a shirt as I meet my brother in the hall.

"You smell like sex," Mason rumbles with a glare.

"I didn't have time to shower." Mason rarely has anything complimentary to say. It's his nature to be dissatisfied. Charlotte is a rare exception and, Mason is completely smitten with his wife.

With good reason, they're perfect for each other. And it's refreshing to see that Mason can soften for someone.

Something I wish I'd seen sooner.

Then again, I'd been so full of anger…

Kim has cleared my head in ways I'd never imagined possible.

"I told you I'd be here at eleven."

"What time is it?" I ask casually, leading the way down the stairs.

"Eleven thirty," Mason retorts. "Which means I got to hear the very loud fuck you just gave my wife's best friend."

"What can I say?" But my skin prickles. I don't want to share any part of Kim. Not even her screams.

"You can say that you're not going to just hit and quit it because I don't want to clean up another of your fucking messes, Leo."

This is how Mason and I end up in fist fights. I should have known it was coming. Mason and I can only play nice for so long.

I spin, my hands clenched. "Thanks for the vote of confidence, bro."

He stops, glaring back. "I was trying to be fine with it. You seemed to be helping her."

I run a hand through my hair as I try to relax. Not fighting with my brother is one of my goals.

"Can we talk about last night and how the Italians came at us again? How they tried to use Kim to hurt us?"

"Right. Good idea," Mason says, pushing past me and entering the kitchen, which is absolutely fantastic.

There's a massive window over the sink, a view of the landscaped back yard, making the space light and airy.

On the island, Mason has a bag of food, which he begins to unpack.

"Look. I've got an idea I want to run by you."

Mason stops. "You're asking for my advice?"

"This is an everyone-in-agreement kind of plan," I say with a deep breath. "And it's definitely more grey than we've been living so..."

The jail time I face for turning over that footage is minimal. But me falling on the sword and killing Toni Carcetti, that time has passed. I need to live my life outside of prison. But I've got another idea, one that works even better than the one I was hatching before.

Mason straightens. I half expect him to shoot me down before I've even begun. "Grey is fine with me. If they're going to come after our women, we'll do whatever is necessary."

I agree.

Taking a deep breath, I start. "We both know that Toni has two daughters."

Mason's jaw tightens. "It's that kind of plan."

"Yeah. And Jake is key so he's going to have to be all in too." I take a breath. "And we might need an assist from the Dukes. They're less known in this town and we might need them to do some tracking and baiting for us."

"Explain."

I do. In quick tones, I tell him my plan that will both protect us and make the kind of move on Toni Carcetti that will cut the head from the Italian snake. I wish I'd been able to implement it before last night. But I'm ready now...

Mason nods as I finish. "It's a good solid plan if Jake agrees."

Again, I'm surprised by my brother's acceptance. "I'll assist him. I'm already on the wrong side of the law handing over that footage."

Mason waves his hand. "That shouldn't be a problem. I've already got lawyers making certain you never see the inside of a jail cell."

"Thanks, Mason," I say, letting out a long breath. "But just in case, we need to discuss Kim."

Neither of us has touched the food he's laid out. Mason grabs a plate from the open shelves, beginning to spoon out food I know he'll barely eat. He's just keeping busy.

I do the same, something about moving, being in action, makes it easier to say some things that need to be said. "If the worst happens, I need to know that you'll take care of Kim."

He pauses, looking up at me. "You know I will."

"I mean like really take care of her. House. Car. Clothes. Security detail. All of it."

Mason sets down his plate. "Okay."

"She's..." I grimace, knowing that Mason's going to freak. But if I've learned one thing, it's that I have to own my shit. "She's pregnant, Mason."

He's holding a serving spoon, his knuckles turning white around the handle. "Are you fucking kidding me?"

"It's mine," I say like that needs to be said. "And so I need to know—"

The spoon flies at my head, and I duck as the metal projectile zings past my ear. "What the fuck, Mason?"

"You got her pregnant," he snarls, coming around the island and I know what's coming. I set down my plate just before he barrels into my mid-section.

I love my brother. And most of the time when we fight, I hold back, because we both know that I'm stronger. Even drunk and on a bender, I never came at him with full force.

But today, I'm in no mood. I can't get beat to shit because I've got a woman to protect.

So as we go flying backwards, I clock him hard in the jaw.

His head snaps back, his teeth clicking together as I land on the marble tile floor, his weight hurtling into my stomach.

It pushes all the air out of me, as we roll away from each other, both of us hurting.

"That's so fucking like you," Mason snarls. "Worried about going to prison while you've got a baby on the way."

Those words fucking hurt way more than what he just did to my stomach. "You think I want to leave Kim? The baby? I'd take the fall because I'm the most natural person to do it and because..." These next words sting my pride but that's been part of my problem...letting pride and selfishness make my decisions. "Because I know that with you and Roman on the outside, we have the best chance of making more money, gaining more power, and that protects Kim and the baby more than me being at their side. I'm ready to admit I'm the least important cog in this machine."

Mason drops his hand, his jaw already swelling, as he stares at me. "Jesus Christ, Leo."

"What?"

"What the fuck have you done with my brother and who is this man?"

Despite the ache in my stomach and chest, I smile. "So you promise? All the protection, all the money?"

"I promise."

"Good. That baby is a Kincaid, Mason. And if there is one thing you've always understood, it's family. I know that I went a little nuts after dad—"

"You think?"

"But we both know I was the one most likely to detonate like he did." I slowly push myself off the floor. "But if I'm going to detonate, I'm going to do it for the good of our family, not for ill."

I hear a soft sob behind me, and I turn to see Kim standing in the kitchen doorway. She's in leggings and an oversized dance sweater that comes off one shoulder.

She looks natural and gorgeous, and I open my arms to her. She only pauses for a second before she rushes into my embrace.

I catch the tears in her eyes as I lift her into my arms. "Don't cry, baby. Everything is going to be fine."

"Do you really feel that way? That the baby is your family?"

"Of course, I do," I whisper into her ear. "I told you this house is yours."

Mason chokes behind me but I know he'll give it to her.

"But I didn't think you meant that the house was really mine."

I look back at Mason, Kim's face buried in my shoulder, and he nods back. I know we're on the same page.

His face is swelling as I lightly set Kim back on her feet. "You should eat," I say. "And I should get Mason some ice."

"All right," she says a moment before she steps away, swiping at her eyes. She takes my plate of food from my hand and digs in with gusto that makes me smile.

My woman can eat my food anytime. I move to the freezer, opening it, and find a drawer of ice. Pulling out some cubes, I plop them in a towel and hand them to my brother.

He sets the ice against his face, his eyes closing. He's going to have a wicked bruise.

"Mason," I start. "One more thing. Does your jeweler make house calls? We're going to need an engagement ring."

His eyes snap open but I don't catch his full reaction because next to me, Kim drops her plate, porcelain and food flying everywhere.

CHAPTER TWENTY-SEVEN

Kim

Food splatters my leggings because...

Is Leo actually talking about buying me a ring?

I'm so glad he thinks of the baby as family. In fact, that alone had my heart thudding in my chest.

But he doesn't have to marry me.

I know that's the least girly thing to say ever, but honestly, the last twenty-four hours have made some things painfully clear to me.

I'm in love with Leo.

It's been there all along, I just refused to acknowledge my feelings. But it's so obvious. It's in the way I can let go of my inhibitions with him. The way he makes my body sing with passion, the way I want to hide behind his very large frame sometimes. The way he makes me feel protected and safe.

And I don't think I could stand it if he married me for the sake of the baby. It makes my heart hurt, just thinking about it.

"Leo."

Mason drops his ice and starts picking up pieces of broken plate from around my feet.

It's a whole different view of the man who has always seemed so cold and distant. There he is, squatted down, shuffling porcelain away from bare feet.

"Yes, baby?"

"We can't get married. I…"

"We can and we will."

"You can't order me to marry you, I'm not some puppet."

"Oh, I know," he steps over the mess, wrapping his arms about me. "I've made some mistakes. Ones that almost really hurt you last night. What I want is to wrap both you and the baby in the protection the Kincaid name gives. Let me do that for you, Kim. Please?"

His words steal my breath. How can I argue with that? But also, I need to think…

Mason stops cleaning, and straightens up, standing next to us before he claps Leo on the shoulder. "I'll have the jeweler come to the house with a wide array. See what Kim thinks of them."

"I haven't agreed to any of this," I say notching my chin, but even I can hear the hesitation in my voice. Despite everything I said, I know there is another part of me that wants to give the baby what I never had. A family with a dad. A father's name.

"Just take a look at the rings, sweetheart. You don't have to promise any more than that."

I swallow down a lump and finally nod. "What time will the jeweler be here? Should I change? I…" I can feel my face heating.

"You look fantastic," Leo says and then kisses me. "Though, you might want pants that don't have eggs benedict on them."

I smile at that. "Right."

"Speaking of, let me fix you another plate. I know you're still hungry." Leo lifts me in his arms to carry me from out of the mess.

"How did you know?"

He smiles at me. "You wake up with an appetite."

I draw in a deep breath as Mason finishes cleaning up the splatters on the cabinet while Leo gets me more food.

Mason takes the dustpan he's found and fills it with debris, dumping it into a trash can. Leo sets another heaping plate in front of me.

"I'll start researching prenatal doctors."

"Roman already recommended one," Leo says as he fills another plate for himself.

"Roman knows already?" I stop chewing my bite of eggs to look at Mason. I can actually hear his hurt feelings. I've always thought of Mason as untouchable. Today is a whole new side of him.

"I wasn't worried he'd take a swing at me," Leo answers, raising his brows.

Mason winces. "I do see the part I play in our dynamic."

Leo gives a nod of acknowledgment. He eats several more bites of his breakfast and then kisses me. "I'm going to go take a shower. You can see Mason out, can't you?"

I nod. Truthfully, I'm glad to have a moment with Mason.

Leo leaves the kitchen and I turn to the head of the Kincaid clan. "Mason?"

"Yeah?"

"I haven't told Charlotte yet and I'd really appreciate it if the news came from me," I start.

He gives me a single nod. "Understood. Though, I have to be honest, Charlotte doesn't let me keep many secrets. Can you tell her soon?"

I smile. "Of course," and then I clear my throat. "Can I ask you a question?"

"Anything."

"This whole thing about Leo and jail?"

He gives me the warmest smile I've ever seen. "Leo has finally become the man he was always supposed to be, and I think you're a big part of that. Trust me when I say that I won't let him leave you now."

My shoulders slump in relief. "Thank you."

Mason crosses to the trash, scraping the rest of his food into the garbage before he dusts off his hands. "I hope you don't mind if I head out, it's another busy day."

"Not at all, thanks for giving me a minute."

His hands go into his pockets. "So…I'm going to be an uncle?"

I shrug, feeling my cheeks heat. "It looks like it."

"Kim, you should know that whether you marry Leo or you don't, you are our family now. You get the full weight of our protection."

Something inside me unwinds. To know that I don't just have Leo, but I have the whole Kincaid brood of dangerously powerful men to help with this child. For the first time since I realized I was pregnant, I don't feel dread or worry. I'm excited. "That means so much, thank you."

He gives me a quick jerk of his chin. "You're welcome. Now, I'm still going to research doctors. Roman's guy is good in a tight spot but maybe not the best source for quality care. Have you started taking vitamins? Exercise?" His gaze skims down me. "Never mind. I know you've got that last piece worked out."

But my brows are slowly rising. There are going to be a lot of cooks in this kitchen. As a person who came from a family of two, I'm realizing it's going to take some adjusting.

I see Mason to the door and then head upstairs to change, just in time to find Leo coming out of the shower, nothing on but a low-slung towel on his hips.

We just had sex. The sight of him shouldn't make my mouth water, but it does.

The man is just so…

He gives me a one-sided grin, and stalks toward me, the sway of his body hypnotic as he crosses the room and then stops to pull me close.

Instead of kissing my lips, though, he plants his lips on my forehead. "Kim."

"Yeah?"

"I know I forgot to ask, but I'd really appreciate it if you'd think about my offer of marriage. I'd like the baby to have my name, but I want you to have it too, baby. Tell me you'll consider the offer."

I nod.

"And if we buy a ring today," His hands splay out on my back, "you can still say no to the proposal, but in my world, wearing that ring is a statement. It makes you less vulnerable."

"I'll wear it," I answer. I've got no fight today. Between all that happened last night, and the multiple rounds of sex, I'm putty in his hands.

He gives me the best smile. Sexy. Sweet, as he kisses my lips. "I'm going to need to meet with Roman, Jake, and Luke. I'll have them here. You rest up while I'm working."

I nod as he disappears in the closet to dress. The checkbook is still on the floor, and I pick it up, looking at the check for twenty thousand dollars. This is my life now?

What will I do all day?

I'll keep dancing. I'll take that class.

As if Leo heard my thoughts, he comes back. "I've got an iPad. If you're bored, feel free to order some furniture. We could use some."

And then he crosses to the desk, pulling out his wallet, and handing me a credit card.

I stare at it, as the cool plastic slides into my hand. "Is today shopping day?"

"I don't think you're furnishing this place in a week."

"How long will we stay here?"

He gives me an inquisitive stare. "As long as you want. Mason understands now, we'll have the deed transferred to our names as soon as the Italians are neutralized."

I look at the card, the check, the house. Just like that, it's all mine. Why does it feel like this can't be real?

CHAPTER TWENTY-EIGHT

Kim

Leo's family arrives, all of the men standing around the island. I disappear into the master bedroom with the iPad and find myself looking at baby furniture.

I know we need couches and tables, but I've never bought any of this stuff and I don't even know where to start.

So instead of buying anything, I call Charlotte.

She instantly picks up. "Kim!" she says by way of introduction. "Did Mason just tell me that you moved with Leo to the burbs?"

"Charlotte," I say, my voice trembling a bit. Telling her is better than telling my mom, but it gets more real when she knows.

Maybe that's why I didn't tell my best friend the other day. Once I do, I need to have figured some stuff out and I need to face someone I love knowing that I made the exact mistake I tried so hard to avoid.

"What's wrong?"

"I..." I swallow down a lump, deciding this is a Band-aid-ripping kind of situation. "I'm pregnant."

My words are met with silence.

"I know. It's the thing I swore I wouldn't do. I lost my head when I met Leo and—"

"Kim," she cuts me off. "Just tell me one thing..." There is a long pause where I feel myself tensing. "Is he good to you?"

I stare at the phone, trying to understand where that one came from. Of all the things I expected Charlotte to say, that wasn't it. "Yes. Why?"

"He doesn't get rough?"

"Never. Why would he do that?"

More silence. "If he ever crosses a line, you have Mason get involved, okay?"

"Charlotte. Leo would never physically hurt me. If anything, he..." He worships me.

"I believe you. It's just, Leo has a dark side and I don't want him to hurt you."

I promise her that I'm fine, but the words unsettle me. Charlotte didn't seem worried about me having a baby nearly as much as she worried about me being with Leo. It wasn't what I anticipated at all and I'm trying to reconcile Charlotte's perspective.

I know there was some stuff that happened between them but maybe it's time I asked some more specific questions.

I'll ask Charlotte but I want Leo's side first. I hear the front door, so I set down my phone and the iPad and head out to the landing.

Roman, Luke, and Jake are just leaving.

Roman looks up at me and gives me a smile and a wave. He looks more like Leo than Mason, which is funny because he acts like Mason. I wave back, feeling my cheeks heat. Do they all know?

Luke nods and Jake salutes. "Welcome to the family," he calls. "Glad I got to see you dance before Leo got his hands on you."

My brows lift as Leo punches Jake's arm. "Don't mind my uncle. He needs a feminine touch."

All the other guys laugh and it's the kind of laugh that you know there is a secret there. I cock my head, assessing all of them as they leave. Guess I don't get to be in on this secret.

Three other men enter, all impeccably dressed, carrying a large case between two of them.

I look down at my clean leggings, the heat in my cheeks growing darker. I should have worn something nicer.

"Set up on the island," Leo says before he trots up the stairs.

He reaches my side and takes my hand. "Ready?"

"No," I shake my head. "I'm not dressed for this."

He leans in and kisses my cheek. "Kim. You are not less than them. You dress how you want to dress, and they wait on you anyway. Get it?"

I am used to people treating me like less, not more. Like I need to dress the part to be believable. "I think it's going to take a bit…"

He smiles. "This will help. Come on."

We walk down the stairs together, one of the jewelers setting out cases, while the other is opening champagne.

"No alcohol," Leo barks out in a clipped tone. The bottle disappears as the man quickly sets up a large light that shines down on the boxes that they begin to open one by one…

I gasp as the rings sparkle in the light, all my reservations forgotten.

Leo pulls me closer. "Diamond? Emerald?" He looks at me, his brows lifting.

"How did you know that's what I like?"

He brushes my cheek, stopping at the corner of my green eyes. "Lucky guess."

Several stones are removed, the diamonds and emeralds are pushed to the front.

I look at several of the diamonds, one simple solitaire making me gasp. The light hits it, the sparkle winking at me from the box.

"Excellent choice," one of the men gushes.

"Excellent taste," another adds. "That's a D-color three-carat solitaire with a VS2 clarity."

I have no idea what any of that means.

But I know this one catches the light like nothing I've seen before.

It's slipped on my finger. I stare down at the stone, my fingers flexing as I hold back a gasp.

Tears sting at my eyes as Leo's hand touches my back. "I'd like to see that emerald as well."

My head whips to him. "You want an emerald for an engagement ring?"

"No," he winks. "It's for your other hand."

My mouth drops open. He isn't serious. Charlotte sparkles with new jewelry every time I see her but she's girly like that.

It's dresses not leggings for her and I just assumed she really liked sparkly things.

But I'm beginning to wonder if the Kincaids just like to drip their women in jewels.

A large emerald of the same cut that's encrusted with side diamonds is slipped on my other hand. It's larger than the diamond, the deep rich color stealing my breath.

"Necklaces?" one of the men asks.

"No," I shake my head.

"I don't see why not," Leo replies.

"Leo!" I straighten. I've conceded a lot of ground today, but two pieces of jewelry is two more than I ever expected to accept. "No more."

He shrugs. "All right. What my lady wants, she gets."

My lips part again as I stare at him.

"So these two?" The man in the center asks.

"That's right. But leave these out. My uncle will be shopping as well."

"Jake is shopping for what?" I ask, now completely confused. I thought Jake was a bachelor for life.

But Leo is already leading me out of the room. "Do they need to be sized?" he asks me instead of answering.

"No." Both rings are a perfect fit.

"Did you make any progress on the furniture front?"

I shake my head. "Every piece of furniture I've ever acquired has been from the side of the road," I say quietly. "I don't have any idea how to furnish a house like this."

Leo pauses before he wraps an arm about my waist. "One piece at a time. Let me see if I can find a tape measure."

Right. We should know what size to get.

An hour later, we're browsing sectionals with price tags that make my head spin.

I'm sitting on the bed, Leo behind me, my body tucked between his powerful thighs.

It's ridiculously comfortable and really fun actually as Leo pulls up a leather sectional. "Too masculine?"

I snuggle deeper into him. "How am I supposed to know?"

He laughs. "I think no dark brown," he scrolls down to a caramel-colored sectional. I point. "What about that one?"

The floors are dark, and the walls a very light cream. "I like it," I say as he reaches over to the nightstand where the credit card sits.

It's then that my phone rings.

It's a New York number so I click the call as I'm scooting off the bed. "Hello?"

"May I speak with Kimberly Evingston?"

"This is she," I smile back at Leo but he's not typing in the numbers, he's staring at me, his expression strained.

"Hi. This is Rebecca Stonefield from the New York Ballet."

"Hi," I answer, my heart beginning to pound. This call is seriously happening now? After everything that's happened this week, now is when the ballet chooses to call?

"We're calling you to offer you a spot on our upcoming roster."

"Oh," I say, swallowing down a lump. "Thank you so much for the opportunity but I've decided to stay in Las Vegas for one more semester."

"Of course," she answers. "That makes sense. I'm sure Mr. Kincaid will be very pleased to hear it."

I hang up, blinking at the phone. Why would the New York Ballet have any idea I was dating a Kincaid?

"Kim," Leo says, his voice holding an edge that makes me physically start. I blink up at him, my stomach churning.

"Why did she think you'd be pleased? Why does the New York Ballet know who you are?"

He grimaces. "Kim."

The sense of dread is building as I lower my phone. "Leo."

He scrubs a hand through his hair. "I'm not proud of some of the things I've done."

My heart is pounding, blood thundering through my ears. "Tell me."

"I…" He's off the bed, coming to stand in front of me. He's everything I know I love in this moment, but I can also feel that I'm going to hate what he says next. That it's another moment where Leo's rash behavior is going to hurt me. "I paid the ballet."

"To what?" I swallow down the lump, feeling dread swell in my stomach.

He looks away, his expression grim. "To delay your acceptance."

I can't even process those words. "Why would you do that?"

"I wanted a little more time with you. Our hook up was so good, I—"

"You ruined my chance?"

His hands come up. "Technically, the pregnancy would have—"

I feel like I'm going to throw up again. "You knowingly and deliberately blocked my acceptance?"

"Delayed," he corrects with a finger. "I—"

"How could you be that selfish?" My voice comes out high and tight. "How could you fuck with my life like that?"

"Kim," it comes out as a plea. "I'm trying to be a better man."

I shake my head. Part of me wants to yell. Scream. Instead, my shoulders slump. "How can I trust you with my welfare or the baby's after you were so callus?"

"Fuck," he spits, and he grabs for my biceps, but I shrug away. "I know I fucked up, okay? I didn't used to be like this and I'm getting back to the man I was. I swear it."

Tears fill my eyes. "I'm pregnant Leo. I've got a baby to raise and that's what you want to say to me. *I think I can do better. I royally screwed up your life, like majorly screwed up your life, but I'm going to give being nice a real go?*" Now my voice is rising, growing high and tight.

I pick up the phone, hitting redial.

"Who are you calling?" He sounds panicked.

Charlotte picks up. "Hello?"

"Charlotte, I need Mason."

Leo plucks from the phone from my hand, hitting the off button and tossing the phone away.

For the second time since I met him, I'm scared. "Leo," I breathe out, but this one sounds different. I can hear the fear in my own voice, feel it tightening my gut. I've never been afraid of him before. Not like this.

Technically, he was hotter under the collar last night at the club. But we were surrounded by people and his irritation was because he was worried about me dancing while pregnant. He was trying to protect me but now…

I feel the shift…

"Do not involve my brother," he grinds out.

"Don't scare me, then." My breath hitches and I realize I've been slowly backing away as he advances.

He stops. "I would never hurt you, Kim."

"You already did."

He scrubs his hands over his face, letting out a feral growl. "I instantly regretted it. I've been wanting to tell you."

"But you didn't." I shake my head, tears finally cresting my eyelashes.

My back hits the wall, and Leo surges froward again, caging me against it. "I had nothing to do with you missing that final."

"I know. But don't you understand? I've never been worth much and—"

"Stop talking about yourself like that!" he roars. "You are everything to me, Kim. Everything."

I blink back my surprise, his words soothing something inside me.

But Leo's not done. "I'm in love with you, Kim. I think I might have been from that very first night. And I've made this habit of getting my way by being a blunt instrument and causing damage wherever I go. When my father died, I just was so angry, I caused hurt everywhere."

He shakes his head, and then, I can hardly believe it, but he drops to his knees. I reach for him automatically, maybe to pull him up, maybe to push him away.

Instead, my hands settle on his shoulders and he wraps his arms about my hips, pulling me close and settling his face against my belly.

"I don't know how to explain that I see it now. What I've been doing wrong. The man I want to be for you and for our child. I'm never going to be Mason, cold and calculating, I'm always going to run hotter than that."

"I like your heat," I whisper. I don't know why I'm comforting him.

"But that doesn't mean that I can't be the man who does what's best for you instead of what is best for himself. Please, Kim. Please give me a chance to prove that." I hear the sincerity in his voice and it guts me.

"I've never asked my mom," I say. "Whether my dad knew about me and he chose not to participate in my life." I squeeze his shoulders. "Do you think he just thought being a dad was too hard? That he couldn't give up his own future for mine?"

Leo's hands are still on my hips but he tips his head back to look up at me.

I softly shake my head. "No one besides my mom has ever put me first, Leo."

I see him wince.

"It's not all the time. And I think when you love someone, you put them first and then you trust that you'll get what you need because they'll do the same for you."

"I know what you're saying, and I know I haven't earned that trust—"

"I love you too, Leo."

His jaw goes so hard, it could cut glass.

"But I'm not sure it's enough."

"No."

"I need to think Leo," I draw in a shaky breath. "And if you love me, you'll let me."

He shakes his head. "If I let you go, you won't come back."

That's when I know. He thinks he's worthless too. And something in my heart melts. I reach for his face and then I lean down and I kiss him. "You don't know that."

"I do."

He wraps an arm around my thighs, lifting me up as he rises. "Why would you come back to the man who stole your future?"

I hold onto his face. I don't want to say too much here. Did he steal my future or replace it with a different one?

"I need to go home. Talk to my mom."

I see the pain that spasms across his face. "I have to let you, don't I?"

"Yes. You can't dictate the terms of how I make choices." And somehow I know, if he lets me go, he's really willing to put my needs first. It will kill him to watch me walk away. But if he does it…

I hear the front door open and close. "Kim?" Mason calls.

I feel Leo tense.

"Up here," I call back.

Leo slowly lowers me to the floor. "All right. You go to Minneapolis. Talk to your mom. But just so you know, I'm calling every day. And I reserve the right to just show up on her doorstep."

This is the Leo I know. Kind even in his strength.

Something in me unwinds and I nod.

"And you're wearing my rings."

I stiffen. "I don't know if that's a good idea—"

"Please," he whispers as Mason appears in the doorway.

I don't answer as I turn away and Leo lets me go…

CHAPTER TWENTY-NINE

Kim

I don't cry in the car as Mason drives me to the airport. I don't cry even when Luke appears at my side at my gate.

"What are you doing here?" I whisper, my eyes darting from him to the flight attendant behind the desk.

"Anthony attacked you, or have you forgotten?" he says with a frown. "You think we'd leave you vulnerable in the airport?"

I frown too. Because he has a point, but it also feels a little like I'm a prisoner. Am I really walking away from Leo when his cousin accompanies me? "And if I decide not to marry Leo?"

Luke shrugs. "Not sure I'd blame you. Leo can be a real prick."

The fact that I want to defend Leo is telling.

But I don't. Because I'm about to get on a plane to Minneapolis where I have to tell my mom that I've been knocked up, and the guy who did it killed my dream to be a ballerina.

But the words fall flat.

Is that even still my dream? Was it ever mine or was it actually my mother's? I didn't feel that much disappointment that I couldn't go. Just that Leo had betrayed me.

Not that Leo's behavior is excused on a technicality. He didn't have knowledge of any of this, nor did he know that I'd become pregnant.

How can I trust a man to be a good father and potential husband when he acted so selfishly?

Luke is in the seat next to me, his eyes closed. "I swear, I can hear the gears grinding in your head."

"What am I going to tell my mom about you?"

"Don't tell her anything. I'll stay nearby where I can keep an eye out without being seen."

"How long are you staying?"

"Until you go back to Vegas, or the Italians are neutralized and not a threat to you."

I cock my head as I look at his profile. I can see the family resemblance. "What was Leo like before his father died?"

"Before he got killed, you mean?" Luke frowns. "He always had a temper. Runs in the family, but he was happy, you know? Sure of himself. But after his dad's death…he fell into real darkness."

When Charlotte lost her dad, she developed OCD that had only just lessoned since she'd met Mason. It was the security he provided that had finally allowed Charlotte to relax and let go.

"Is that why Charlotte's afraid of Leo? I know they went out a few times. Did she see that darkness?"

Luke looks at me. "Charlotte didn't tell you?"

I shake my head. We both like to play things pretty tight to the chest. It's one of the reasons we work so well as friends.

Luke scrubs at the back of his neck. "Mason and Leo were at odds for a long time. Leo was looking for reasons to lash out and Mason is so rock solid, he made a good target. Mason doesn't flinch and he took a lot of Leo's anger. But when Charlotte became involved…"

I think I understand. Leo's anger at Mason spread to Charlotte, only my friend isn't rock solid. She's fragile.

"It was never about Charlotte, though. Leo never cared about her. He just wanted another reason to really hit Mason hard. I think he was angry that Mason wasn't more emotional about the loss of their father. And that Mason kept it together when Leo fell apart."

I turn forward, thinking back to that night in the club when Leo came in blustering about my dancing.

This whole time, I have to be honest, I've been wondering why Leo would want me. I believed my stupid ex, that I wasn't worth much.

But suddenly, I realize that I don't let Leo get into that space where he loses it. I pull him back. Maybe it's by kicking him in the shin, or by hugging him.

Even in our bedroom this morning. He pulled it back...

I sit up straighter, feeling valued. Feeling worth something. I like helping people, I always have. And Leo might need me as much as I need him.

Luke and I take most of the rest of the flight in silence.

He rents a car after we land and drives me to my mom's apartment.

It's worse than the last time and I stare at it wincing. "Jeez," I softly whisper under my breath, wondering what Luke thinks about her place.

He's scanning the street. "Leo is not going to like this at all. We're going to have to move your mom."

I turn to Luke, my mouth opening. "Your protection extends to my mom?"

"Well, you'll come to visit, won't you?" Luke says, stepping out of the car to come open my door.

He does, helping me out before he grabs my bag. "You want to go anywhere, you call me."

I take the bag from his hand with a nod. He holds the handle, not releasing the bag. "What do you think you're going to do about Leo?"

I shrug. "He scared me this morning."

Luke gives a nod. I appreciate that he doesn't try to convince me of anything. "Growing up, Leo was my best friend. Still is."

"Even the past few years?"

"They're the exception. Not the rule. And honestly, he's coming back. I see it. If somebody shot my dad right in front of me, I'm not sure how I'd handle it either."

"Oh," I whisper. How come no one told me that part? That Leo was there? How would I deal with watching my mom die like that?

Luke lets my bag go and I start for the door. Luke watches me make my way to the front door with its four bells. I know my mom is in apartment C and I ring the bell, hearing her footsteps on the stairs in the house.

She opens the door, opening her arms wide. I step into her embrace, my insides unwinding.

It makes me think of Leo. He doesn't get to have this. No one loves you like a parent…except for maybe a spouse.

I wave to Luke and then step inside, the stale smell of the hall curling my nose.

My mom brings me up the stairs into her place.

There are boxes everywhere, and the furniture can't disguise chipped and cracked plaster.

"That's some hardware you're wearing," my mom says as she steps into the kitchen, immediately opening the fridge to pull out food.

"Hardware?"

She gives my hands a pointed look.

I plunk down into one of her kitchen chairs. "I'm technically engaged."

"Technically?"

I look down at the diamond which catches the light even in the single bulb that hangs over my mom's table.

"Can I ask you a question?"

She stops chopping lettuce to turn to me. "Sure."

"Did my dad know you were pregnant?"

I see my mom swallow. "He did."

A dull pain radiates through me. "So, he chose not to love us?"

My mom turns back to the cutting board, grabbing a tomato to slice. "We were both young. He was going to college. I…"

"Did he ever call? Ask?" I fiddle with the ring.

"A few times."

"Ever give you money?"

"No," my mom sighs. "He married, started a family of his own."

"I see." I don't. Wasn't I his family?

"Why all these questions now?"

"I'm pregnant, mom." It's easier to just put it out there and as nervous as I am for her response, I feel better for pushing the words out.

"And your boyfriend proposed?" She goes back to the fridge, pulling out some chicken.

"He did," I answer with a deep breath. I don't want to tell her about the ballet, or about Leo's questionable lifestyle. Instead, I focus on myself. "But marrying would mean never being a ballerina, I think." I thought giving up that dream would hurt more. But it doesn't at all.

My mom stops making sandwiches, sliding into the chair across from me. "And what do you want?"

"Leo and I haven't been dating that long." I know I didn't answer. "What if he's not the right guy for me?"

"The fact that he asked is a major point in his favor."

I nod. Because my mom is right.

And barring calling the ballet when the two of us had known each other for all of a few hours, he's been nothing but supportive since.

I wince as I think that. "You're not upset that I won't get into a major dance company?"

My mother shakes her head. "Of course not. Did you go to college to be a dancer?"

"No."

"I assumed you had different dreams when you chose UNLV."

"But all you ever talked about was my potential." I'm staring at her, and she has the decency to wince.

"I wanted you to be more than me, Kim. More than this," she waves her hand at her derelict place. "Comfortable. Happy. I don't care if you're a dancer, a teacher, an administrative assistant. I just wanted you not to struggle the way I did."

My heart breaks a little. Because Leo definitely takes the financial struggle out of my life. "How do you know a guy is right for you?"

My mom shakes her head. "You're asking me? I'm not exactly an expert."

I smile, my chin dipping as I get up from the chair to finish making our sandwiches. "Right."

"But I think you pick the guy that makes you feel best about you."

I pause over those words because I don't have to think much to know that no man has ever made me feel more valued and treasured than Leo. And no man has ever made me feel so needed either.

My phone dings where it sits on the table and I glance back, seeing Leo's name.

I pick it up, swiping the phone open, but the message makes me gasp out a breath…

CHAPTER THIRTY

LEO

A CASINO IS the last fucking place I want to be tonight.

I watched Kim walk out the door this afternoon and it took everything in me not to hold her back. But I have got to stop holding on so tight. It's one thing to get angry. It's another to manipulate the people you care about and try to control them. I see the line and I have to learn not to cross it.

That's what I lost somewhere along the way.

It became this zero-sum game where control was the only thing that mattered. When I really think about, it makes sense.

Losing my dad was this incredible moment where I was in control of nothing. But that can't extend to the people I care about.

I can't hold them in place for my own personal gain. It's not going to work and I'll only push them all away.

Not that any of this applies to tonight. Because one thing I intend to control fully and completely is my plan to keep my family safe.

Jake and I take my usual booth in the corner at the Diamond Casino, a water sitting in front of me as Jake sips a glass of bourbon.

"You're really drinking tonight?" I say as I take a sip of my Perrier, my bad mood making me dickish.

"Just because you quit doesn't mean the rest of us have to."

"I'm not suggesting you quit. Maybe just not drink tonight, considering what we're here for."

"Why we're here is exactly why I need to drink," Jake snarks back. "I can't fucking believe I agreed to this. I'm a confirmed bachelor, you know. This is a no-commitment package," he waves at himself.

I scowl. "Are you sure that's your choice? Maybe no woman wants your ugly mug."

He takes a large swallow of his drink. "You're confusing me with you."

That hurts more than it should, and I punch his arm hard. He takes the hit with a grunt. "You've always had fists like anvils."

I look down at my phone, checking to see if Kim responded to my text. Still nothing.

I read back through the message I sent her hours ago, telling her how much I loved her. Telling her how I'd quit the clubs and move to New York, be daddy day care if it meant that she'd marry me.

I was hoping for some kind of response.

I let out a frustrated growl. I want my woman back. I don't care what I have to give of myself to get her back at my side and back in my bed.

"Would you stop sulking over your phone," Jake grouses. "She's not calling tonight."

I set the phone down with more force than necessary. "I know that."

"Then what are you so pissed about?"

"I'm pissed that I'm an unlovable fuck up," I grit out. "She should hate my guts. I'm a complete dick."

Jake sets down a drink. "You're only a partial dick."

"Thanks," I answer, taking a large swig of my water.

"So am I. So is Luke, and Mason is a complete bossy prick."

"You're a real fucking poet, you know that?" But I relax back into my seat. "We all know that I'm the worst of us."

Jake shakes his head. "No one had to do what you did. You had a right to go haywire, Leo. We don't talk about it but..."

I shake my head. "I don't want to talk about it now."

Jake gives a slight nod. "We all know you needed time. It's what you do next that determines the type of man you are. Not what you've done in the past."

Those words make me pause and I pick up my phone again.

A message pops up, but it's not from Kim. It's from Charlotte.

Two pictures come through, one of Kim dancing and another of sunlight shimmering off her hair.

They make my chest hurt.

Thought you might like these. Is Charlotte's message.

"Charlotte's a decent sister-in-law," I say as I stare at the second photo.

"She's perfect for Mason," Jake concedes. "But tonight is about me...and your plan. And if I'm not mistaken, that's the British prick, Griswold Smith."

I turn in my seat, catching the gaze of a dark-haired man with the sort of looks that might make me and my brothers look ugly.

He gives me the barest nod before he pivots toward the bar. And that's when he approaches a stunning blonde.

I mean, stunning. That is the thing about all my hours spying in this joint. Toni never kept a regular schedule but a few other members of his family did.

"Shut the fuck up," I say.

"No one was talking," Jake answers, but his voice sounds strained. His head dips. "Least of all me. She's going to be so disappointed when I'm the one she's stuck with."

I should attend his words more. There's meaning there I don't understand. But I'm busy looking at the woman Griswold has approached. "She's not going to have a choice."

"That can't be Antonia Carcetti," he whispers. "Toni Carcetti is an average looking dude at best. How can that be his daughter?"

"She goes by Nia." I say, taking another sip of my water. "And she's Toni's daughter. I'm sure of it."

I stare, sinking deeper into the shadow of our corner table.

Jake clears his throat, his knuckles white around his drink. "When you asked me to do this, you didn't tell me she was so beautiful."

I give my uncle a hard stare. "It doesn't change anything." I've seen Toni's older daughter, she doesn't look anything like Nia. Maybe she would have been an easier target for Jake, but Nia is Toni's favorite, and this is about making the boss of the Italian Mafia really fucking hurt.

Gris is chatting with Nia, leaning close, whispering in her ear. She's blushing a little, I can see it from here. "I guess you're not going to try and charm her because you'd never beat that Brit. He is so good looking, he makes me uncomfortable."

"Fuck you," Jake spits at me through clenched teeth. Then he's up and headed toward the door. I don't follow, watching the Brit flirt with Nia, brushing her hair over her shoulder and skimming his hand down her arm.

She gives him a breathless smile before he takes out his phone and hands it to her. She's giving him her number…perfect.

He leaves a minute later, doing a lap around the room before he heads for the exit. I follow, taking the direct route, but I keep my head down. We're in Italian territory here and I'm not trying to cause trouble. At least not tonight.

I exit, making my way out the front door and down the street by the parking garage where I find Jake and Gris already talking.

Jake is furiously tapping a cigar I know he wants to light up. But he doesn't. Good for him.

"I did as you asked," Gris says in his slick accent. "Set up a date for next Friday night. Group thing. Her friends. My brothers. I'll keep it gentlemanly and then make another…"

The Dukes have been promised the bones of the Italians so they are exceptionally motivated to make this plan work. "Just remember, the second date you send an Uber to pick her up. Make up any reason you want."

"I'm aware of the plan," Gris says. "And I'll text the date in advance and then a fifteen-minute warning. Don't worry. This is going to be like taking candy from a baby."

"In this case, the baby is a murdering Italian, which means nothing is easy...I promise you that," I add into the conversation. "You take care to make certain this doesn't come back to you."

Gris turns to me. "You're the one who got both Vendetti and little Anthony in prison?"

I jerk my chin in affirmation.

"If you say it then, I believe you. I won't underestimate Toni. But to be honest, I think what my brothers and I are more concerned about is which Italians we'll be dealing with when Toni is dethroned. Whoever they are, they're not going to take kindly to us buying out their casino dirt cheap."

For once, I don't even think about his words. That will be Mason's job, not mine. And I'm glad it's not mine. No jealousy, no malice. Mason will be better at that than me. My job is to take out the enemies threatening our family. I am the fist. And Toni Carcetti is going to feel my punch. Hard.

And after that, I'm going to be supporting Kim during her pregnancy whether she wants to be with me or not. Hopefully with me, but either way, I'm hers to command.

Gris leaves and I turn back to Jake. "We've got a few weeks before this all goes down. I think I might make a quick trip to Minneapolis."

Jake grimaces. "You sure? Maybe what you need to give that girl is space."

"You're not wrong," I answer with a sigh. "But I'd also like the chance to prove to her that I'm ready to be whatever she needs. It's not about me, it's about her."

"Where is my nephew, Leo?" Jake asks, pushing my shoulder.

I know what he means, but the truth is, I feel more like myself than I have for a very long time.

Now, I've just got to convince Kim that I can be the man she needs.

CHAPTER THIRTY-ONE

Kim

I read Leo's text a hundred times over the course of the evening, his words and my mother's pinging in my head.

Finally at about midnight, lying on my mom's couch, I lift my phone to type a response.

I miss you.

It's simple, it doesn't make promises. Drawing in a deep breath, I hit send.

My phone rings almost instantly.

I shake my head. Patience is never going to be Leo's virtue.

"Hello?"

"It's late, baby, you need your sleep."

I smile. "I'm on my mom's broken-down couch. It's not very comfortable. Which means I'm not likely to sleep." The truth is, though, that I've just been thinking about him. Thinking about all the things he's done for me since that one time that he didn't act in my best interest.

"I can get you a hotel room."

I shake my head. See. That's the Leo I know. "No. It's okay. I've got to help my mom anyway."

"With what?"

"She's always rented her dance studio. We moved to a million different apartments, but the dance studio was always constant. She told me tonight that her landlord is retiring, and he sold the strip mall. The new owners aren't renewing her lease, and she has to move her business."

Silence meets my words. "Can I help?"

"I don't think so," I answer automatically.

"Real estate is actually something my family excels at, you know."

I smile into the phone. He's not wrong. "It's less about real estate and more about money. She hasn't got any."

More silence meets my words. I know what he wants to offer but I can't take his money for my mom. Things are convoluted enough.

I hear him draw in a deep breath. "Just tossing out an idea...wherever we move, if we go together, maybe your mom could come too. That way you'd have family besides me. Might make you feel more secure with me being me—"

"Leo," I sit up with a cry, my throat clogging. Because that is an offer that doesn't just throw money at me. It's personal, and with a baby on the way, it's exactly what I need.

"What's wrong, baby? Did I upset you?"

"No," I feel my eyes welling. These pregnancy hormones are a killer. "It's perfect, actually. It's exactly what I need."

"We could all move to New York," he starts. "And in the meantime, we've got a guest house here," he offers up. "She'd be right on the property without being able to hear how I make her daughter cum—"

"Leo!" But in the background of the call, I hear an intercom. "Wait. Where are you?"

"The airport."

"Why? Where are you going?" I feel panic rising. Where is he off to and how long will he be gone and how far away will he be from me? It's one thing to think of him waiting in Las Vegas for me to return when I'm ready.

"Don't be mad."

"Why would I be mad?" My worries replaced with suspicion as my eyes narrow and I sit up straighter.

"I was thinking of following you." He says quietly. "I know you haven't made up your mind, but I didn't want to sleep in that house without you. You don't have to see me, but I want to be close, and I won't pressure you I promise—"

"Leo," I whisper into the phone, relief, not irritation pulsing through me.

"Yeah, baby?"

"Just get here already," I say with a smile. "And I'll pitch moving to my mom in the morning. You get a hotel room. We're definitely not sleeping on this couch together."

"I sleep anywhere you are, Kim. I mean it."

My smile grows. "Me too. Turns out, I can't sleep without your chest as a pillow."

He chuckles. "That's because I'm comfortable."

He is. And his strength makes me feel safe. I want his body next to mine. "I went to my mom's studio this afternoon."

"Yeah?"

"It's the most comfortable place in the world to me besides being with you," I say with a sigh. "I don't think I want to be a professional ballerina, Leo." I swallow down a lump. "I think I want to be a teacher. Open a little studio of my own. What do you think about Henderson? Seems like a good suburb for it."

"Seriously? You want to stay in Vegas?"

"I do. I want to be with you, and I want our baby to grow up with a big family. Not like mine."

I hear his silence. "Baby?"

"Yeah?"

"Hang on a minute? My plane is boarding."

"Okay," I answer, disappointed. Did he not like my plan? I hear the attendant in the background speaking to him and then it goes quiet again.

"I guess I want you to know that I meant my offer. We can go to New York."

My insides melt. "I can't even imagine the hours and dedication it would take to recover from the baby and then be a professional dancer." Something is shifting. My mom worked three jobs because she had to, there weren't any choices. But I've got them. "I think I know what kind of mom I want to be and that's the kind that's around for the kindergarten plays and the first dance recital or little league game."

But it's more than that. "And if I'm honest, I took a hard look at why my dreams have always been what I thought I needed to prove to the world that I was worthwhile. And maybe to my father, whoever he is..."

"Your father?"

"Yeah. I'd envision this moment where we'd meet and I'd be like, my mom could have been a professional ballerina, you know, that woman you didn't want. But she raised me, and I ended up being the professional dancer because she was right to keep me, and you could have been part of this."

"Sweetheart," Leo sounds pained.

"I know. It's raw. But I need you to know that it matters to me that you'll be there, Leo. That you're going to stick with us."

"I'm sticking, baby. Don't you worry. Where you go, I go. Including Minneapolis. Speaking of, the flight attendant is glaring. I'm not used to flying commercial and I think I'm pissing her off. I think I need to hang up."

I almost smile at his words. "Okay. But you'll be here tomorrow?"

"I'll be there. Get some sleep."

Amazingly, I do. The moment we hang up, I'm out, and when I wake, I hear my mom softly speaking from the kitchen.

I open my eyes and Leo is sitting at her tiny kitchen table. He looks ridiculously large in this place.

I gasp as I vault off the couch.

He turns and stands in one fluid move, catching me in his arms.

Wrapping my arms about his neck, I kiss him several times. I don't stop until my mom clears her throat.

"Promise me the next time we fight, we can stay home?" he chuckles into my ear.

My mom's place isn't great for makeup sex. I kiss his neck. "I'm going to run to the bathroom and then maybe we'll head out for breakfast?"

He gives me a squeeze before setting me down. "Mom, we're probably going to hang for the day, Leo was up all night so he needs some sleep, but how about we all do dinner tonight?"

She gives me a wink and a nod as I collect up my stuff, brush my hair and change my clothes.

I'm assuming we're going back to the hotel to eat, shower, and go to bed, all of which I'm down for.

Where and how many times we make up is the only question on my mind as Leo takes my hand and leads me out to his rental car. A Toyota Camry.

I'm used to his sports car so I stop, my brows lifting.

He sighs as he opens the door for me. "They didn't have anything else and I thought I might as well get used to a sedan. A baby seat is not fitting in the back of my 911."

"You're thinking of car seats?"

"Did you know that the Camry has some of the best crash-test ratings?"

I slide in, marveling at the man who comes around to the driver's side.

He sits in the driver's seat, adjusting the review mirror before he starts the car. "I have to be honest," I say, turning to him. "I've never found a guy driving a Camry hotter."

He puts on his sunglasses, giving me a sexy grin. "Well get ready, cause we're about to do thirty-five through this whole town."

I laugh as he starts up the GPS and then leaves my mom's street.

Noting the route, I tap his shoulder. "We're going to go right by my mom's studio. Mind stopping? I'd love to show it to you before it's gone."

"I don't mind at all," he answers.

Two minutes later, I'm pointing out the turn and we're parked in the back of the studio.

I know where my mom hides the key, it's been in the same spot for twenty years and a minute later, we're in the familiar space.

This is where I lived my life and I breathe in the scent of aging wood as we walk down the narrow hall past the office and bathroom and into the main dance room. It's a decent space with mirrors on the back wall and a bar attached for the girls to use. I step up to it now, slipping off my ballet flats as I do a few kicks, warming up my legs.

Leo comes in behind me. The whole front of the room is windows out to the parking lot, but my mom pulls curtains across them to lower the air conditioning costs in the summer and they're closed now.

In my bare feet, I spin about the room, humming to myself as I dip and sway. Not like a cage dancer, but as the ballerina I've been trained to be since the age of two.

"You've never looked more beautiful," Leo murmurs when I finally stop.

I smile at him.

"You're sure you don't want to go to New York? I can be a stay-at-home dad. I bet I could rock reading time at the library."

I stop, staring at the man I know I love. "I can see it now, all the stay-at-home moms hitting on you," I wrinkle my nose. "We'll take turns going to the library, how about that?"

"I like it," he murmurs before he pushes off the wall.

"And I'm sure I want to stay in Vegas. Charlotte is there. Your family is there and tonight, we'll pitch my mom the idea of moving too. Maybe we can even open that studio together."

"Another family business?" He stops right in front of me, wrapping a hand around me to cup my ass in his palm and pull me close.

But I don't want to talk about my mom anymore. My hips press to Leo's and I can feel his already stiff cock rubbing me right where I need it most.

CHAPTER THIRTY-TWO

LEO

KIM TWIRLING around this studio is the most beautiful thing I've ever seen.

Part of me wanted to watch longer but I can't keep my hands off her. Because not only is she perfect, she's mine.

One of her hands comes around the back of my neck, her fingertips massaging my skin as her chin lifts up so that I can claim her mouth with a kiss.

I kiss her like a man who's been starved. I have been…for her. My hand is still wrapped around one of her ass cheeks and I give it a good hard squeeze, pulling her even tighter into my hips.

She responds by wrapping one of her legs around my waist.

"I love you," I murmur against her lips. I'm not normally a sentimental guy during sex. I'm far more of the make-the-walls-bang, but I can't help it with her.

I thought I might lose her, and it scared the shit out of me. To have her here against my body, emotion is welling up inside me.

This is exactly where I belong. Wherever she is with her body pressed to mine.

Which is why I growl out a protest when she takes a step back. But my irritation is quickly forgotten when she pulls off her shirt, revealing a lace bra underneath.

And then she takes three more steps back until she's leaning against the bar, half reclined with her eyes on me. "Your turn."

Giving her a cocksure grin, I tug my shirt off. I haven't showered yet today but neither has she. I'd planned on a two-for-one back at the hotel room. Sex in the shower.

But as I catch her reflection in the mirror behind her, I think this is a better plan. I'm going to watch Kim as I fuck her senseless and then I'm going to take her back to the hotel and thoroughly clean her in the shower.

And likely fuck her again.

Because this is my woman.

I kick off my boots, pulling at the button of my jeans before I shuck them down my thighs.

My cock is already at full attention as I stand, legs spread wide, arms crossed in the center of the room.

I watch her gaze slide down me as she nips at her bottom lip and swallows. "You're so powerful, Leo. I don't think I'll ever get used to all those muscles."

"You will, baby. These muscles are yours." And then I start walking toward her. "Yours for protection..."

I stop just in front of her. "Yours for carrying the burdens of life."

"What else?" I see her reach to unclip her bra.

"Car seats. I can carry those."

She smiles as the bra slips down her arms.

I'm reminded of that first night at the wedding when I had her against the wall. I drop to my knees, hooking the waist band of her leggings and pulling them down her thighs. "I'll be great at moving couches."

She laughs then as she buries her fingers into my hair. "I bet you will."

"I'll carry you, Kim. In whatever way you need." And then, her leggings still around her knees, I lean forward, sliding my tongue between her thighs to give her clit a little lick.

Her legs buckle, and I grab her hips in both my hands, holding her up as I lick deeper, eating Kim like she's breakfast.

Because she's delicious.

Both of her hands are in my hair now, pulling at the strands as she whimpers in pleasure. I like her little cries, but I love it when she screams.

Using one of my forearms to hold her weight, I use my other hand to part her lips and then slip a finger inside her pussy, her slick heat making me even harder as her folds contract around me.

Fuck, I love feeling the inside of this woman.

She's clenched so tightly around me, her legs trembling, I know she's not going to last much longer.

I push another finger inside her, my tongue working at her clit as I suck her lips into my mouth.

She lets out a scream, her body convulsing in an orgasm that makes her wilt over me, her belly coming to my head.

But I'm not even close to done.

Yanking the leggings the rest of the way off her body, I lift her up and take a step back.

Her legs naturally come around my waist. From a few feet away I have an amazing view of her back and ass in the mirror, but even better, spread like this, I see her little asshole and her red, swollen lips as my cock slides through them.

I lift her a few inches, angling my hard-on and then plunge inside her.

From the mirror, I have the perfect view of the way she swallows my cock, the thickness of it, disappearing inside her as she arches back to take even more of it in.

"I look like I'm going to break you in half," I grunt out, loving what I'm seeing.

"You're not," she gasps back. "You feel so good, Leo."

Hands on her ass, I slide her up and then plunge her back down on my cock, watching as I move out of her and then back in.

She rolls her hips, her ass out. The bend of her body is that of a dancer and it's beyond hot.

I pump into her several more times, my hands on her ass only spreading her wider for my view.

I know I'm not going to last long. The past few days have been so raw and this woman is turning into my entire world.

Her head is thrown back, her neck exposed, and I lean down to suck one of her tits into my mouth, pulling her nipple so that she cries out my name. I feel her tighten around me and I know she loves it. But I miss the view.

So lifting my head, I take her in again.

Her body swallows my cock over and over and it's so good, I close my eyes for a second.

And then, shifting her weight to one hand, I slide my middle finger through her soaking pussy before I slide it into her tight little asshole.

I feel her stiffen, her body stilling.

"You all right, sweetheart?"

"I'm good."

"You sure?" I want to claim every part of her, but not if it robs her of pleasure.

"Sure." She relaxes and takes even more of my finger in, and I watch in the mirror as I fill both her holes pumping in and out of her like a man half mad.

Her face is red, the little noises she's making almost guttural, but she grows tighter and tighter around my finger and cock, her hands gripping my back like I'm a lifeline.

"Are those good noises or bad ones," I ask, squeezing my eyes shut a few times to clear the red haze from my eyes. I could lose myself in fucking her like this.

"Good," she cries. "So good. Leo. I don't think I can make it much longer."

Fuck me. I pump harder, ruthlessly, every muscle flexing as I push so deep inside her, she lets out another keening cry.

Her nails drag down my back, her legs locked so tight as she pushes down on me, taking so much of me in that my vision blurs.

And then she starts to cum.

It's not like her first orgasm. Those cries were pretty. These keening cries pierce my ears as she absolutely breaks apart on me, her pussy locked so tight, I start to cum before I've even had an orgasm. It's like she's pulling the cum from my cock.

"Fuck," I spit as she slams down hard on me again, riding the pleasure for every last bit it's worth.

My orgasm hits me with a force that sends me to my knees, not that I stop pumping her so full of my cum, her thighs are going to be sticky for days.

It goes on and on, the force of it, emptying my balls. "Christ. No wonder you ended up pregnant."

She laughs a halfhearted breathy sound, as her forehead comes to my shoulder. "Leo. That's not funny."

"I wasn't trying to be funny. You know how to empty a man of every drop of cum."

Her palms slide down my arms. I'm on my knees but I'm still holding her up. "We've got several months to work out the birth control issue."

"Fuck that," I say, sitting my ass down on the hardwood. She's still got her legs around my waist.

She pushes back to look at me. "We're not having sex after the baby?"

"I asked you to marry me. Of course we're having sex. I just don't plan on wrapping up."

Her eyes go wide.

"I've thought about it, and I think I want a bunch of kids."

Her mouth falls open, her eyes so wide that I can't help but lean forward to kiss her lips closed.

"A bunch of kids?"

"What do you think of five?"

"Five?" she croaks, shaking her head. "Putting a finger in my ass makes you want to have kids?"

"That's just a side perk, baby." I push her hair back from her face... with the other hand. "You're a good girl, Kim, who is only dirty for me. Which is why I plan on asking again and again for you to be my wife and have a bunch of my babies."

She shakes her head and then leans her forehead back on my shoulder. "Yes."

"Yes, what?"

"Yes, I'll marry you. I seriously doubt I'm having five babies."

"Four?" I grin, kissing her long and hard.

Because Kim just agreed to be my wife. And she's having my baby.

I don't feel anything other than beautiful gratitude. This is exactly where I'm supposed to be, and she is the woman I'm meant to be with.

And for the first time in a very long time, I understand my purpose, my drive, my whole reason for being.

And it's fucking beautiful.

EPILOGUE

JAKE

I FOLD MY HANDS, sitting forward in my seat as Kim makes her way down the aisle toward Leo.

Not that I recognize my nephew.

I mean, he looks mostly the same. Bulging muscles, large frame, big white teeth in his smile.

Only everything else is different.

Leo normally carries this edge of anger…it rolls off him in waves, lashing out at everyone and everything he passes.

But just like that…it's gone.

In its place, is a wide-open joyous smile, as Leo extends his hand to the woman he's marrying.

His eyes are light and filled with joy, as he bounces on the balls of his feet.

Leo is fucking bouncing.

I frown, trying to decide what I think about all of this. We're in the midst of a war and one of our most fierce soldiers is grinning and bouncing.

But beyond that, I can't deny that I'm happy for him.

Kim is pregnant with his baby, not that she's showing at all. As a dancer, she's still as slender as ever.

She reaches him and he pulls her into his arms, kissing her long and hard.

"Ahem," the Justice of the Peace clears her throat. "The kissing is supposed to happen at the end of the ceremony."

Leo's grin only widens. "Don't worry. There will be plenty of kissing then too."

The small crowd laughs.

Next to me is Luke, my nephew, Leo's cousin. He's got the same thick muscles and normally surly disposition that Leo's got.

He's smiling as he watches. "You ever see Leo happy like this?"

"Never." Which isn't totally true. Before the Italian Mafia killed my brother, Leo's father, Leo was happy a lot.

And somehow, Kim has brought him back to that man. It might almost make a crusty old-school asshole like myself believe in love.

Nah.

That's for other people who can afford it. And I don't mean money. I can afford whatever I want. Kincaid Enterprises is worth billions and as one of five Kincaid men, I'm an equal share owner.

I have always been tougher, meaner than my nephews. I grew up with an old-school father who was fond of using the whip and he had no trouble bringing me into business when our family was dirty.

Not like it is now.

Mason, my oldest nephew, makes our money nice and legal. I've got to hand it to him, he's done a good job.

But there's a few dirty jobs left, and one of them is getting revenge on Toni Carcetti. The man who killed my brother.

Leo came up with the plan to get the job done before he went completely soft.

But now it's on me to see it through. Leo's got Kim wrapped in his arms as he says his vows. The man is so deeply in love, it's completely obvious...

Leo isn't the man for this job.

"I promise to love, honor, and cherish you until death do us part." His deep voice echoes over the backyard of their new home.

A mansion in the swankiest district in Vegas, the pool sparkles in the morning sun.

Across the aisle, Kim's mom sits in a chair, Kim's roommates dabbing at their eyes.

One of them, a leggy brunette, makes eyes at me across the way. I think her name is Kendall or something.

I turn away with a barely covered snort.

I don't get mushy enough at weddings to fuck some chick because I caught some feelings.

I don't have feelings. At least not those. I've never been in love and as I'm pushing thirty-five, I think I'm a pretty baked cake. So I seriously doubt I'm ever falling in love.

Now, you might be able to sell me on taking advantage and screwing one of these women who's got bride envy.

Except, I'm smart enough to know that messing with one of Kim's friends is a choice that is likely to bite me in the ass.

And I can get tail anytime I want.

So I sit back in my seat, listening to Kim repeat her vows, Leo grinning like a complete fool as she says them.

Christ.

He's making me a little nauseous.

He's already bought a crib even though Kim isn't due for months and earlier this week he invited us over to assemble it.

I'm just this side of a gangster. I don't assemble baby gear.

I drank scotch and sat in the nursing glider, because, honestly, those chairs are comfortable.

Might get one.

Has a foot stool that glides too.

But I digress. Anyway, we set around with tiny stupid Allen wrenches and discussed how we were going to bring down the head of the Italian mafia here in Vegas. Not two activities you'd expect to go together.

Then again, considering the first part of this plan Leo has concocted, it's probably fitting.

I'd sipped my scotch and rocked in the glider as I'd watched Leo hunched on the floor.

Behind him were boxes of vibrating chairs, which are an interesting idea, and exer-saucers, complete bullshit if you asked me. And I'd asked the questions one last time. "You're sure she's a witness in the murder?"

"If Melissa was telling the truth, then yes." Melissa is Leo's former club manager and a backstabbing bitch, so her information is suspect in my book.

"And what if she's lying?"

"Either way, Nia is his favorite. Taking her will be your leverage to get him to confess."

I grimace remembering the next part of my plan, my attention focusing back on the ceremony in front of me.

I've been to a few weddings.

None of them have ever been like this. There are only about fifteen guests here, our family, Kim's mom and roommates, and a few business associates.

"I now pronounce you man and wife. You may kiss your bride."

"Finally," Leo roars and then pulls Kim tight against him, kissing her with a whole lot of tongue.

I let out a long breath. Today is going to be a nauseating day.

Kim and Leo come back down the aisle, and we all rise, clapping for the new couple.

I have to hold back a sigh, enthusiasm is not in my emotional repertoire.

But I do smile as they reach the end of the aisle, and Leo picks up his new bride, not stopping to greet guests. Instead, he just keeps walking right into the house.

Kim lets out a small cry of protest but the men around me all chuckle.

"He doesn't want to wait to have sanctioned sex," Luke says from just behind me. "I can appreciate that."

"He's an emotional guy," Roman chuckles from the next row.

I cock my eyebrows. "When you're married, does wanting to bang your wife count as emotion?"

They all laugh at that as I catch the eye of Gris Smith, an Englishman who is part of another major family in Vegas. They call themselves the Dukes, and we've made a deal with them that if they can help us out with this plan, they'll be able to acquire some choice Vegas real estate when the Italians are forced to sell it.

Gris jerks his head toward the side yard and then starts walking.

I follow, sure he's got something he'd like to discuss.

We disappear around the house, leaving the rest of the guests behind. "Gris," I give him a nod. "News?"

"It will be tonight," he says with a quick dip of chin.

"Tonight?" A bit of regret lances through me. We've gone through great pains to make all this happen, but there is a part of me that hates this plan no matter how beautiful Nia Carcetti is.

Nia is Toni Carcetti's daughter, and the apple of his eye.

Gris Smith approached her at the Italian's casino and secured a date. The man is so handsome, he looks fake. And the Dukes are still relatively unknown in Vegas, which means Gris was able to fly under the radar.

He took Nia out on a group date, and then another. A few of his friends, a few of hers. Perfect gentleman both times.

He altered the original plan, but he says Nia is really skittish. Which makes sense. Toni keeps his daughters on very tight leashes. They aren't allowed to date.

But Gris, slick fuck that he is, has convinced Nia to sneak out. Tonight.

That's where I come in.

Gris hands me a set of keys with an H emblem. "A Honda?" I grumble, holding out the keys like they smell bad.

"Uber drivers don't do pick-ups in Maseratis." He slaps my shoulder. "You're going to love the Accord. Roomy interior."

I snort.

From inside the house, a loud banging against the wall interrupts our meeting. We both look up, knowing that Leo is screwing his wife against the wall.

"He's got some serious thrusting power," Gris says appreciatively, even as the chorus of Kim's cries join the banging.

"Kim certainly thinks so," I answer back.

Gris covers his smile with his hand. "Right. So, I'll text you as soon as I tell her that I can't pick her up because I'm running late and that I'm sending an Uber."

That's me. I'm the Uber. Only I'm not taking her to her date.

I'm taking her to a place in the desert and then I'm going to convince her to betray her father and marry me.

Yeah. If you're thinking that I might lack the charm for this, you'd be right. But I'm going to have to dig deep and find a way.

And use every piece of information we've been able to glean to hopefully persuade her.

Because Toni Carcetti is going down and his daughter, Nia, is going to help me whether she likes it or not.

WANT TO READ MORE? King of Wrath

BONUS EPILOGUE

Bonus Epilogue:
Leo

One year later...

I should be asleep. It's been in short order these days, and I should be catching up where I can, but I'm too wired to sleep.

Our little baby Abigail got her days and nights mixed up for close to a month. After a few days, Kim looked like a zombie.

That's when we taught Abigail to use a bottle, and I took over half the night duty.

I'm used to late nights at the clubs, so I send Kim to bed early and then Abby and I hang out until two or three in the morning before Kim takes over.

She's older now, four and half months, and sleeping better. But I still take care of the first feeding.

I love this time.

It's dark, it's quiet, and Abby is the sweetest thing that has ever existed on this entire planet. Except, of course, for her mother.

Abby's got dark hair and dark eyes, but the doctor says that can change as she gets older. I'm hoping she's a redhead like Kim.

Currently, Abby is lying against Kim's side, tucked in the crook of her arm. It's so beautiful that as I lie next to them, I can't make myself close my eyes.

I love this life.

I love it so much that my heart contracts painfully in my chest.

Kim's eyes flutter open and she gives me a soft, sleepy smile. "Everything all right?" she whispers as she shifts Abby closer.

I brush her hair away from her face. "It's great."

"It's late," she sighs. "You must be exhausted."

Maybe I should be. I'm back to work at the clubs, though I'm paying the managers to do most of the night duty. I come home for dinner and bath time, and a few mornings a week I go in late to do daddy/daughter things. Tomorrow, we're going to story time at the library. All of us. For some reason, Kim doesn't want to send me by myself with Abby.

"You can sleep in tomorrow," she says her eyes closing again. "Abby won't notice if you miss the library."

"Nah," I say. "We'll go. You could stay home, though. Mama can take a nap or get in a workout." Kim has been dancing to get herself back in shape.

"You sure? I don't mind coming."

"I've got this. I've already picked out her outfit. I got her that pink dress."

"Pink dress? Who are you and what have you done with my husband?"

I wink. "I've got to get her ready for dance class with grandma."

Kim and her mom opened the studio, but Kim only teaches one morning a week and every other Saturday. She doesn't even look like she's had a baby, and my biggest parenting challenge has been to not wear Kim out with how much I want to fuck her all the time.

I can't help it.

I show my sentimentality with a good bang.

And if I'm being honest, after having Abby, my life makes complete sense in a way that it never did before. This is exactly where I'm supposed to be.

I'm already trying to convince Kim to have another. She's resisting but I figure, the more I do with Abby, the more babies I can convince her to have.

I wasn't joking. I swear, I was meant to be a dad. I'm going to spend the rest of my life taking care of my family.

I can't imagine a better future.

Kim's eyes close, but she tucks Abby into her body and rolls so that she's spooning Abby and I'm spooning her.

I wrap my arm around both of them, holding them close, keeping them safe. I nuzzle my nose into Kim's neck, breathing in her scent.

I already feel myself relaxing into sleep. This is where I'm the most comfortable. Snuggled up with my girls.

STALK ME LIKE AN ALPHA!

Join my newsletter to get all the latest updates!

Tammy's Newsletter

And follow me everywhere else for teasers, giveaway, book news and fun!

www.authortammyandresen.com
www.facebook.com/authortammyandresen
www.instagram.com/tammyandresen
https://www.tiktok.com/@lordsoflasvegas
www://amazon.com/authortammyandresen

MORE ABOUT TAMMY

Tammy is the writer of Bestselling Regency Romance who could not resist the urge of writing in the dark and delicious world of Contemporary Dark and Steamy Billionaire Romance.

She lives with her husband and three children in Massachusetts and her favorite adventures are the ones that are found in books but occasionally she lives a few of her own!

Made in the USA
Monee, IL
14 September 2025